ANNE

MURDER IN MIMICRY

ANNE Morice, *née* Felicity Shaw, was born in Kent in 1916.

Her mother Muriel Rose was the natural daughter of Rebecca Gould and Charles Morice. Muriel Rose married a Kentish doctor, and they had a daughter, Elizabeth. Muriel Rose's three later daughters—Angela, Felicity and Yvonne—were fathered by playwright Frederick Lonsdale.

Felicity's older sister Angela became an actress, married actor and theatrical agent Robin Fox, and produced England's Fox acting dynasty, including her sons Edward and James and grandchildren Laurence, Jack, Emilia and Freddie.

Felicity went to work in the office of the GPO Film Unit. There Felicity met and married documentarian Alexander Shaw. They had three children and lived in various countries.

Felicity wrote two well-received novels in the 1950's, but did not publish again until successfully launching her Tessa Crichton mystery series in 1970, buying a house in Hambleden, near Henley-on-Thames, on the proceeds. Her last novel was published a year after her death at the age of seventy-three on May 18th, 1989.

BY ANNE MORICE
and available from Dean Street Press

ANNE MORICE

MURDER IN MIMICRY

With an introduction and afterword by
Curtis Evans

DEAN STREET PRESS

INTRODUCTION

BY 1970 the Golden Age of detective fiction, which had dawned in splendor a half-century earlier in 1920, seemingly had sunk into shadow like the sun at eventide. There were still a few old bodies from those early, glittering days who practiced the fine art of finely clued murder, to be sure, but in most cases the hands of those murderously talented individuals were growing increasingly infirm. Queen of Crime Agatha Christie, now eighty years old, retained her bestselling status around the world, but surely no one could have deluded herself into thinking that the novel *Passenger to Frankfurt*, the author's 1970 "Christie for Christmas" (which publishers for want of a better word dubbed "an Extravaganza") was prime Christie—or, indeed, anything remotely close to it. Similarly, two other old crime masters, Americans John Dickson Carr and Ellery Queen (comparative striplings in their sixties), both published detective novels that year, but both books were notably weak efforts on their parts. Agatha Christie's American counterpart in terms of work productivity and worldwide sales, Erle Stanley Gardner, creator of Perry Mason, published nothing at all that year, having passed away in March at the age of eighty. Admittedly such old-timers as Rex Stout, Ngaio Marsh, Michael Innes and Gladys Mitchell were still playing the game with some of their old élan, but in truth their glory days had fallen behind them as well. Others, like Margery Allingham and John Street, had died within the last few years or, like Anthony Gilbert, Nicholas Blake, Leo Bruce and Christopher Bush, soon would expire or become debilitated. Decidedly in 1970—a year which saw the trials of the Manson family and the Chicago Seven, assorted bombings, kidnappings and plane hijackings by such terroristic entities as the Weathermen, the Red Army, the PLO and the FLQ, the American invasion of Cambodia and the Kent State shootings and the drug overdose deaths of Jimi Hendrix and Janis Joplin—leisure readers now more than ever stood in need of the intelligent escapism which classic crime fiction provided. Yet the old order in crime fiction, like that in world politics and society, seemed irrevocably to be washing away in a bloody tide of violent anarchy and all round uncouthness.

Or was it? Old values have a way of persisting. Even as the generation which produced the glorious detective fiction of the Golden Age finally began exiting the crime scene, a new generation of younger puzzle adepts had arisen, not to take the esteemed places of their elders, but to contribute their own worthy efforts to the rarefied field of fair play murder. Among these writers were P.D. James, Ruth Rendell, Emma Lathen, Patricia Moyes, H.R.F. Keating, Catherine Aird, Joyce Porter, Margaret Yorke, Elizabeth Lemarchand, Reginald Hill, Peter Lovesey and the author whom you are perusing now, Anne Morice (1916-1989). Morice, who like Yorke, Lovesey and Hill debuted as a mystery writer in 1970, was lavishly welcomed by critics in the United Kingdom (she was not published in the United States until 1974) upon the publication of her first mystery, *Death in the Grand Manor*, which suggestively and anachronistically was subtitled not an "extravaganza," but a novel of detection. Fittingly the book was lauded by no less than seemingly permanently retired Golden Age stalwarts Edmund Crispin and Francis Iles (aka Anthony Berkeley Cox). Crispin deemed Morice's debut puzzler "a charming whodunit . . . full of unforced buoyancy" and prescribed it as a "remedy for existentialist gloom," while Iles, who would pass away at the age of seventy-seven less than six months after penning his review, found the novel a "most attractive lightweight," adding enthusiastically: "[E]ntertainingly written, it provides a modern version of the classical type of detective story. I was much taken with the cheerful young narrator ... and I think most readers will feel the same way. Warmly recommended." Similarly, Maurice Richardson, who, although not a crime writer, had reviewed crime fiction for decades at the *London Observer*, lavished praise upon Morice's maiden mystery: "Entrancingly fresh and lively whodunit. . . . Excellent dialogue. . . . Much superior to the average effort to lighten the detective story."

With such a critical sendoff, it is no surprise that Anne Morice's crime fiction took flight on the wings of its bracing mirth. Over the next two decades twenty-five Anne Morice mysteries were published (the last of them posthumously), at the rate of one or two year. Twenty-three of these concerned the investigations of Tessa Crichton, a charming young actress who always manages to cross paths with murder, while two, written at the end of her career, detail cases of Detective Superintendent "Tubby" Wiseman. In 1976 Morice along with Margaret Yorke was chosen to become a member of Britain's prestigious Detection Club, preceding Ruth Rendell by a year, while in the 1980s her books were included in Bantam's superlative paperback "Murder Most British" series, which included luminaries from both present and past like Rendell, Yorke, Margery Allingham, Patricia Wentworth, Christianna Brand, Elizabeth Ferrars, Catherine Aird, Margaret Erskine, Marian Babson, Dorothy Simpson, June Thomson and last, but most certainly not least, the Queen of Crime herself, Agatha Christie. In 1974, when Morice's fifth Tessa Crichton detective novel, *Death of a Dutiful Daughter*, was picked up in the United States, the author's work again was received with acclaim, with reviewers emphasizing the author's cozy traditionalism (though the term "cozy" had not then come into common use in reference to traditional English and

American mysteries). In his notice of Morice's *Death of a Wedding Guest* (1976), "Newgate Callendar" (aka classical music critic Harold C. Schoenberg), Seventies crime fiction reviewer for the *New York Times Book Review*, observed that "Morice is a traditionalist, and she has no surprises [in terms of subject matter] in her latest book. What she does have, as always, is a bright and amusing style . . . [and] a general air of sophisticated writing." Perhaps a couple of reviews from Middle America—where intense Anglophilia, the dogmatic pronouncements of Raymond Chandler and Edmund Wilson notwithstanding, still ran rampant among mystery readers—best indicate the cozy criminal appeal of Anne Morice:

> Anne Morice . . . acquired me as a fan when I read her "Death and the Dutiful Daughter." In this new novel, she did not disappoint me. The same appealing female detective, Tessa Crichton, solves the mysteries on her own, which is surprising in view of the fact that Tessa is actually not a detective, but a film actress. Tessa just seems to be at places where a murder occurs, and at the most unlikely places at that . . . this time at a garden fete on the estate of a millionaire tycoon. . . . The plot is well constructed; I must confess that I, like the police, had my suspect all picked out too. I was "dead" wrong (if you will excuse the expression) because my suspect was also murdered before not too many pages turned. . . . This is not a blood-curdling, chilling mystery; it is amusing and light, but Miss Morice writes in a polished and intelligent manner, providing pleasure and entertainment. (Rose Levine Isaacson, review of *Death of a Heavenly Twin*, *Jackson Mississippi Clarion-Ledger*, 18 August 1974)

I like English mysteries because the victims are always rotten people who deserve to die. Anne Morice, like Ngaio Marsh et al., writes tongue in cheek but with great care. It is always a joy to read English at its glorious best. (Sally Edwards, "Ever-So British, This Tale," review of *Killing with Kindness*, *Charlotte North Carolina Observer*, 10 April 1975)

While it is true that Anne Morice's mysteries most frequently take place at country villages and estates, surely the quintessence of modern cozy mystery settings, there is a pleasing tartness to Tessa's narration and the brittle, epigrammatic dialogue which reminds me of the Golden Age Crime Queens (particularly Ngaio Marsh) and, to part from mystery for a moment, English playwright Noel Coward. Morice's books may be cozy but they most certainly are not cloying, nor are the sentiments which the characters express invariably "traditional." The author avoids any traces of soppiness or sentimentality and has a knack for clever turns of phrase which is characteristic of the bright young things of the Twenties and Thirties, the decades of her own youth. "Sackcloth and ashes would have been overdressing for the mood I had sunk into by then," Tessa reflects at one point in the novel *Death in the Grand Manor*. Never fear, however: nothing, not even the odd murder or two, keeps Tessa down in the dumps for long; and invariably she finds herself back on the trail of murder most foul, to the consternation of her handsome, debonair husband, Inspector Robin Price of Scotland Yard (whom she meets in the first novel in the series and has married by the second), and the exasperation of her amusingly eccentric and indolent playwright cousin, Toby Crichton, both of whom feature in almost all of the Tessa Crichton novels. Murder may not lastingly mar Tessa's equanimity, but she certainly takes her detection seriously.

Three decades now having passed since Anne Morice's crime novels were in print, fans of British mystery in both its classic and cozy forms should derive much pleasure in discovering (or rediscovering) her work in these new Dean Street Press editions and thereby passing time once again in that pleasant fictional English world where death affords us not emotional disturbance and distress but enjoyable and intelligent diversion.

Curtis Evans

The author wishes to thank Jonathan Marks for his invaluable guidance on points of law and police procedure in the district of Columbia

PART ONE

CHAPTER ONE

ON THE day after he was promoted to Chief Detective Inspector, which happened to coincide with our fifth wedding anniversary, Robin and I treated ourselves to a celebration lunch in Soho, at the conclusion of which he proved once more how worthy he was of his new eminence by striding off in a southerly direction, bolt upright and with as steady a gait as if he had been lunching off steamed fish and soda water. This left me to make my solitary, very slightly weaving way round the corner into Dean Street and to stagger even more laboriously than usual up the three murky flights of stairs to my agent's office, where I had an appointment at three o'clock.

I mention these circumstances only as a reminder of how one thing can so often lead to another, for it must be said that if Robin had not been promoted to Chief Detective Inspector, but demoted to Sergeant and we had actually lunched off steamed fish and soda water, I should not have been airily signing my name on a dotted line which led straight to a six months stint in the United States, within ten minutes of our renewing our marriage vows and swearing never again to part. On the other hand, if it had not been for that celebration lunch, we should still be making do with the same, worn out drawing-room carpet and I should never have made the acquaintance of lovely old Inspector Meek of Homicide, so life would have been impoverished in one way or the other and it is no use trying to re-write the balance sheet now.

However, to put events into their correct sequence for once, when I lurched into my agent's office, grinning like a lunatic, she said:

'Hallo, my darling, so you got here at last! Lovely to see you! Do sit down, you look as though you might have scarlet fever rather badly.'

This friendly greeting was echoed in less fulsome terms by my cousin, Toby, whom I dimly perceived to be occupying the chair by the window, thereby adding to the general sense of unreality, since Toby could rarely be coerced into visiting London in any circumstances and does not belong, in the professional sense, to my agent. They are not even particularly good friends. It soon transpired, however, that his presence on this occasion was directly connected with my own, and for the following reason:

Toby's most recent comedy, *Host of Pleasures*, now nearing the end of its London run, was soon to be transferred to New York, a deal for the American rights having been made by Messrs. Schenk and Pattison, and this had made it necessary to re-cast two of the parts. Catherine Fuller, the leading lady, had opted to go to America, but, owing to some rather complicated tax arrangements which necessitated his being domiciled in Switzerland, Roger Bellamy, who played opposite her, had elected to stay at home. The other change concerned the second female lead, since the actress who played it had become pregnant during the run, and it was this which was now being cast at my feet. Not pearls before swine, however, for I had both seen and read the play a number of times and had no doubts about my suitability for the part, which in fact had been conceived with myself in mind. The fact that I had been obliged to turn it down, for domestic reasons, mitigated my guilt in accepting the offer now, for on the first time around the rehearsal period had clashed with Robin's first chance in two years for a real holiday and he had set his heart on a safari-like jaunt in Kenya.

This time, having agreed, there was no turning back and my agent, who had stayed her hand until the die was cast, then plied me with black coffee and details of the schedule, which were as follows:

The newly formed company would rehearse for two weeks in London, starting on 3rd September, thereafter to disperse and later reassemble in Washington for a further three-week rehearsal period. The play would open on 15th October at the Eisenhower Theatre in the Kennedy Center, where we had a month's engagement before moving into New York.

All this was such music to my ears that I felt a perverse compulsion to find at least one wrong note in it: 'Only three weeks?' I enquired.

'More than enough,' Toby assured me, 'you appear to forget that most of them have been working together for months, even the understudies.'

'No, I hadn't forgotten, but they'll be in strange surroundings, just as much as me. Three weeks on a stage none of us has set foot on before doesn't sound an awful lot. What about lighting, for a start?'

'Really, Tessa, you are not required to be director and stage manager as well, you know. All we ask is that you should learn your part like a gallant little trouper; and I daresay they have a few lights knocking around somewhere in the Kennedy Center, and someone who knows how to switch them on and off.'

'Don't rise, my darling, don't rise!' my agent implored me, 'they've got Marty Jackson for the lighting. He's madly experienced and knows the Eisenhower like the back of his grubby little hand.'

'Oh, good!' I said, forgetting to sound dubious, 'I love Marty, he's such a dear.'

'I am so glad you approve,' Toby said, 'I am sure we all want the SS *Eisenhower* to be a happy ship. Any other little matters you'd care to sort out while you're here?'

It was tempting to reply that my only remaining worry was how to break the news to Robin, but did not envisage this going down very well, since nothing is more unpopular than the kind of unprofessionalism which intrudes domestic problems into working life and I was aware that this was one canoe which I should be required to paddle on my own.

All the same, the dilemma was still uppermost in my mind when Toby and I descended the dark and dirty staircase to Dean Street and this, combined with the blinding shock of emerging into the glare of afternoon sun, caused a moment or two of delayed reaction when we were hailed by a tall, willowy, middle-aged man alighting from a grey Rolls-Royce, which was blocking the street from end to end, and looking the very picture of a Shaftesbury Avenue duke in his sporty tweed suit and hat. It was only when he had pushed the latter to the back of his head, in order to facilitate the embraces, and had greeted us both in a clear tenor voice, which also had the effect of riveting the attention of every individual within a radius of twenty yards, that I came out of a dream and recognised him.

'Gilbert was very cordial,' I remarked to Toby when, the full spate of endearments having washed over us, he and I continued our leisurely progress towards Leicester Square, 'considering that he's supposed to hate your guts, by all accounts.'

'Not any more. That hatchet is now buried. Or, at any rate, a handful of soil has been thrown over it.'

'That's good news. A dangerous enemy, so they tell me.'

'But a valued friend?'

'That would imply that he had some.'

'You're very hard on poor old Gilbert. Is the champagne turning sour on you, or have you other grounds for dislike?'

'Nothing personal, but he played a very lousy trick on a friend of mine, who happened to be three-quarters up the creek at the time. Gilbert put the boot in. Apart from that, I only know him by reputation and one can hardly say fouler.'

'An omission which is about to be corrected.'

'What a depressing thought! Why should you think so?'

'I know so. Gilbert is our new lead. He is taking over from Roger and you'll be rehearsing with him at ten o'clock on Monday week.'

'You're joking, Toby!'

'Not at all. He may not be your own favourite, but American audiences hold a different view. In fact, his name alone ensures a sell-out for the entire run at the Kennedy before we even open.'

We strolled on in silence, crossing Coventry Street and making for Trafalgar Square, my heart or some adjacent piece of anatomy growing heavier with every step. The ordeal of breaking my news to Robin had grown lighter in comparison with this new onslaught from Fate and the burning emotion now was one of resentment against Toby and my agent for having, as I saw it, conned me into committing myself when not in full possession of the facts. The only slight consolation was that, for all Toby's complacency, as he preened himself on the fame and fortune which awaited him on the banks of the Potomac, he would eventually come to realise that no matter how successful his play might become in the experienced, manipulating hands of Gilbert Mann, it would be unrecognisable to anyone who had known it before, including its progenitor. Unfortunately, what I could not foresee was that by the time this came to pass it would not only be the play which had undergone a sea change, but every single person connected with it as well.

CHAPTER TWO

ROSE Henneky, our principal understudy was already seated in the non-smoking section when I boarded the plane at Heathrow, but the smokers were in the minority on that trip and after take-off she moved to a seat on the aisle across from mine, which allowed us to talk when we felt inclined to and to pretend not to have heard one another when the interest flagged.

On balance, I was glad of her company, for Rose, although rather a whiner, was an undemanding sort of woman and I had begun to feel lonely and homesick before we were even over Bristol, though I confess that the first sight of her dim, prim and trim figure had added substantially to the queasiness which always accompanies the knowledge that three thousand miles of solid ocean lie between me and my destination. No blame attached personally to Rose for this, but it was an undeniable fact that her career, which covered a quarter of a century in the theatre, had been notable in only two respects. One was that everyone who worked with her found her easy to get on with, the second that her presence invariably spelt bad luck. When this Jonah's mantle had first fallen on her frail shoulders I could not say, since it had already become a legend before my time, but I could recall half-a-dozen tales of scenery being sent to the wrong town, stage hands downing tools, the star of the piece collapsing with a heart attack and, on one celebrated occasion the theatre she was playing in had literally been burnt to a cinder between the matinée and evening performance.

Luckily for Rose, if not for all of her colleagues, this reputation was more than offset by the patronage of Catherine Fuller and there was good reason to believe that so long as Catherine lived and worked Rose would never want for a job.

They had been close friends for many years, having met when Catherine was playing Lady Teazle in a short-lived revival and Rose, in addition to a walk-on part, had been given the understudy. There was little physical resemblance between them, but this had been of no consequence in a costume play and any objections it may have given rise to later had been firmly over-ruled by the great Catherine. The friendship had survived that production and dozens more which followed it, and in each of them Rose had been her understudy.

Nor was their relationship confined to the theatre, for they also shared a flat in Eaton Square, two cairn terriers and a weekend cottage near Aylesbury, where, contrary to the predictable pattern, it was Catherine who toiled away at weeding the garden, exercising the dogs and cooking and catering for their regular Sunday luncheon parties. Rose was more apt to spend these recreational periods reposing in a darkened room, recovering from the exertions of a week doing nothing in the theatre, or else grappling with one of her chronic migraines. However, despite the unfair division of manual and material contribution, they appeared to exist in a state of bickering, but well founded understanding and although each had collected a husband or two along the way and, in Rose's case a son as well, who had inevitably gone to the bad, all these encumbrances had now been discarded and they depended solely on each other. Or so I and everyone else believed.

'Katie flew out the day before yesterday,' Rose explained, in answer to the unspoken question. 'We both hate air travel, so we're better apart. She went ahead to fix up the apartment we've rented. Dear old Katie, never happier than when she's organising things.'

'Where is your apartment?'

'On New Hampshire, quite close to the theatre. It's one of those service places, with everything laid on, including two kitchen sinks, so there really shouldn't be a single tiny thing to do, but Katie's idea is that we should have most of our meals at home and I expect she's busy stocking up the fridge. They offered us a suite at the Watergate, which would have been more convenient in a way, but somehow neither of us quite fancied the idea.'

'I agree with you. It was suggested to me too, but I was afraid it would give rise to a certain uneasiness.'

'And the demon king is staying there, which also rules it out, so far as we're concerned.'

'Which demon king?'

'Gilbert. Hadn't you heard Katie's name for him? She maintains that if he ran out of tricks for upstaging he'd be perfectly capable of making his entrance through a trapdoor in the stage, preceded by a sheet of green flame. The name has rather stuck. Where will you be staying, then, Tessa?'

'Oh, I've been lucky. A friend of mine lives in one of those dreamy little houses in Georgetown and she's offered to put me up. At least, I'm not absolutely sure whether I'll be staying with her, or living there on my own. She travels a lot and she also tends to get married and divorced rather frequently, so her movements are subject to circumstances beyond her control. Still, she's promised to try and be there for at least part of the time. It doesn't matter terribly because I know where to find the key and there's a maid who comes in three mornings a week to tidy up.'

'But not living in?'

'Oh no, it's only a tiny place. Two bedrooms.'

'Then I certainly hope you won't have to be there on your own,' Rose said primly. 'One hears such tales.'

'Yes, I know, but I think they mostly apply to the raffish down-town areas. Georgetown isn't a bit like that; more of an urban reservation for the well heeled and well behaved.'

'That may be, and no doubt it's safe enough once you're indoors, but it's quite a step from the theatre and personally I wouldn't fancy it, specially late at night. That's the main reason why Kate and I have settled for this service flat. It's not a particularly attractive way of life to be eating and sleeping and working in one tiny area, but at least we'll be able to lay on a reliable taxi to bring us home every night. I think you may find there are disadvantages in being so far afield.'

This was one remark I pretended not to have heard, for I have noticed that no sooner do people embark on a course of action which they do not find wholly satisfactory than they muster every argument to persuade others to imitate it, which in this case I had no intention of doing. Fortunately, I was able to slide out of the discussion quite easily because a steward had now stationed himself between us and was flogging sets of plastic ear phones in readiness for the post luncheon film show.

A few minutes later Rose reopened communications, though luckily on a different topic.

'Hugo's on this plane,' she said. 'Did you know?'

'No,' I replied, craning my neck to peer ahead of me and then at the seats behind.

'Oh, not in here, he's travelling tourist. He wangled an exchange on the ticket and put the difference in his pocket, wouldn't you know? Just the sort of little dodge that would occur to our Hugo.'

'Is he really as hard up as he claims?'

'It's hard to see why he should be; no wife nowadays, no dependents at all, so far as one can tell. He's just congenitally mean, if you ask me,' Rose said, turning down the corners of her mouth as though she had bitten into a quince filled with strychnine. 'He'd travel in the luggage compartment, if they'd knock off fifty pounds.'

Hugo Dunstan, to whom she so disparagingly referred, occupied a parallel position in the hierarchy to my own. Gilbert Mann and Catherine Fuller shared top billing, which is to say that their names appeared side by side and in large print above the title, while Hugo's and mine, also on a level, were in smaller type below it, the two remaining members of the cast taking the line below that. These were Clive Lea and his opposite number, Jacqueline Cortot, a tempestuous beauty, with thick dark hair and thick legs, to mention only two. They played a young married couple on the brink of divorce and in real life were a young married couple, passionately and volubly in love.

These technical details may seem trivial to the public for whose benefit the billboards are displayed, but are of the highest importance to those whose names appear on them and few people felt more keenly about this than Hugo, who was possessed by a gnawing ambition, principally, if his reputation was anything to go by, in order to amass vast riches, for at this stage in his career he was celebrated for nothing so much as his meanness.

Appearances were deceptive however, for, far from creeping around with a lean and hungry look, he was a hearty and jocose young man, with a facetious manner and a great penchant for practical jokes. He had a rare talent for mimicry and was not a bad comedian either, although too much inclined to mouth and strut and too often guilty of slowing down the pace with heavy, farcical mime, in his efforts to wring every last titter for one of his lines. This failing had already earned him some scathing rebukes from Gilbert and for once I was on Gilbert's side, although as most of my own scenes were played with Hugo I could be said to be prejudiced.

'We shall have to be very careful when we land,' Rose was now saying, 'and pretend we haven't seen him. Otherwise, he'll try and scramble into our taxi and scrounge a lift. American cabs are quite uncomfortable enough without Hugo bulging all over us. I'm assuming you won't have a car to meet you?'

I shook my head: 'Not unless Lorraine turns up in hers, which I doubt. She's, got a very ancient M.G. but she doesn't use it more than she can help and anyway, if she is in Washington, she'll be working during the day.'

'Then we may as well share. It's a twenty dollar ride into town, as you probably know, and no point in shelling out a double fare. And if you'll accept a word of advice, Tessa, I suggest you come to our apartment and telephone from there, to make sure your friend is at home. It will give you the chance to make other arrangements if she's not.'

Bossy old Rose! I thought to myself in some astonishment. I had never previously conversed with her at such length, except in the presence of Catherine, when she always appeared so meek and cowed, and this unexpected domineering streak made me wonder if the back seat she habitually occupied, both in her public and private life, was really of her own choosing, or whether she was stuck with it out of necessity.

In any case, these were certainly her own personal views that she was foisting on me, and not those handed down from her mentor, for when my situation was explained to Catherine she displayed a remarkable indifference to the hazards it might present.

Catherine Fuller was probably nearing sixty by that time, but still at the height of her success. She was not quite so tall as she appeared on stage, but above average and her height and slenderness were accentuated, as always, by her lovely, elegant clothes. Her thin, veined hands looked too fragile for the heavy rings they were always loaded with and her fine, pale hair was piled into a bun on the crown of her head, from which a number of coils and tendrils had escaped and were hanging over her ears and forehead. All very carefully contrived, no doubt, but the effect, as usual, was admirably casual and pretty.

'And aren't you lucky, my darling child?' she asked in her fluting, contralto voice, 'Georgetown is quite fabulous, isn't it? All those adorable eighteenth-century houses and little pink pavements! I quite wish we were living there ourselves.'

'Oh, but Miss Fuller, this is such a gorgeous apartment,' I protested in gushing tones. No one, apart from close friends, and contemporaries, was permitted to call her Kate and a fair amount of gush did not come amiss either. Not that much effort was required to produce it on this occasion, for it genuinely was a gorgeous apartment, in a style which Americans manage so well, full of pale polished surfaces contrasting with colourful rugs and enormous, blissfully comfortable sofas, and one entire wall composed of sliding windows, opening on to a spacious, green carpeted balcony, with a view right over the flat roof of the Kennedy Center to the Potomac, flanked by trees which at this season were in their full autumn glory.

'Rather characterless, you know,' Catherine replied, giving each syllable its due. 'Inoffensive enough, in its way, but one has the feeling that if one were to walk into any of the other flats in the building, it could be days before one discovered one's mistake. And now, my dearest Rose, I positively insist that you go straight off for a good long sleep.

I'm convinced that the only way to get over this jet lag is by total surrender. You'll do the same, Tessa, if you know what's good for you.'

'I really don't feel in the least tired, darling,' Rose protested with a reversion to her tremulous, petulant manner, 'it was quite a painless trip and it seems a sin to spend such a lovely sunny afternoon in bed.'

'There'll be another one tomorrow and you'll enjoy it much more if you take my advice, believe me. I'll call down to the desk for a taxi, Tessa. They're very efficient about that, but they'll want to know exactly where you're going. I can't tell you why, but the drivers apparently insist on being primed with every detail in advance.'

'1312A Erskine Lane,' I told her, 'between P and Q, North-west, if they really want it all.'

'How perfectly charming! And Tessa's bound to live up to it, don't you agree, Rose? No one has prettier manners.'

It has to be confessed though that they weren't always so impeccable as she gave me credit for. After a few minutes there was a call on the house telephone to say that my taxi was downstairs and when I had been bustled out, with stern warnings not to keep it waiting, I paused for a moment outside the apartment door, checking through my purse to make sure I had plenty of change, and remained there with my eyes closed and my ears strained to catch Catherine's voice, which I heard uplifted on the other side of the door.

'. . . praying for her to go,' I heard her say, '. . . can't ever tell you what the wicked demon . . . effrontery . . . begins to look—'

It was too good to last, of course, and unfortunately Catherine's impatience to unburden herself had not inter-fered with her priorities, for there came a low, murmuring reply from Rose, followed by Catherine's voice again, still recognisable, but sounding now as though it came from the bottom of a well and, realising that they had moved into another room, I had no choice but to let good manners reassert themselves and to continue on my way.

CHAPTER THREE

1

As ANYONE who has been to Washington will know, it is not a large city in terms of population, but covers such a vast area that a journey from one part to another can often include half-a-dozen contrasts in landscape, going the whole way from wooded countryside to garish downtown shops and cinemas, and there is ample space for all the historic buildings and monuments to remain inviolate in their original settings, safe from the encroachment of urban developers. The result, while impressive, lacks cohesion and is also slightly provincial. However, since this visit marked my first acquaintance with it, the only thing I knew was the way to the Kennedy Center and I had made up my mind to profit by the knowledge without further delay.

Conceivably, if I had not been so pushed around by my two managing, middle-aged ladies, nor bundled off their premises quite so summarily, personal inclinations would have coincided more closely with Catherine's recommendations, but the need to assert my independence, combined with a new lurking fear that I would not find Lorraine at home, and the house taken over by marauding gangs of drug sodden rapists and murderers, gave me the courage to tell the taxi driver that there had been a misunderstanding about my destination and that, if it would not mean breaking too many rules, I would be grateful if he would first drive to the Kennedy, now clearly visible in all its slab-cake glory and, if possible, wait there while I went inside to deliver a message.

Surprisingly, in view of Catherine's warnings, he made no objection whatever, saying it was okay to park there on a Monday and that I could take my time. As a matter of fact, he looked alarmingly like a drug sodden, murdering rapist himself, having a very wild look in his fierce black eyes and wearing, for some unfathomable, but doubtless sinister reason on this warm afternoon, a scarlet woollen cap, like a giant egg cosy, pulled down over his ears. However, I was determined to brave it out and, keeping my fingers crossed that he and my luggage would both be there when I returned, I sped down the side of the building in search of the stage door.

Approached from the city, the Eisenhower Theater is the first of the three main auditoriums which are housed in the Kennedy Center complex, the other two being the Opera House and the comparatively modest and intimate concert hall. I had been told that the Eisenhower seated over a thousand people and, having never before performed in a theatre anywhere near that size, was anxious to get an advance taste of the horrors in store and also to discover, if that should prove possible, something about the lay-out of the dressing rooms.

For once, the stage door was not at all hard to find and the interior also differed dramatically from any I had seen before. It opened straight on to a spacious, carpeted foyer, very streamlined and chastely decorated, with a reception desk facing the entrance and rows of pigeon holes on the wall behind it. There was no one in attendance, but over to my right was an archway, leading to a similar sized room, from which the sound of a typewriter being pounded to a pulp hit the ear like a friendly, welcoming rattle. I walked through to investigate and found, as I had hoped, that the

typist was Terry Rack, our company manager. It was a measure of my growing sense of isolation that I found myself
regarding him with deep affection, for in the normal way
Terry was far from being my ideal, chiefly owing to his
incurable amateurism. He had taken up and abandoned
numerous careers before coming to roost in the theatre,
including social welfare, public relations and receptionist
at an art gallery and seemed destined to move, before very
long, to yet another venture, being somewhat starry eyed
about his own abilities and equating frenzied activity with
high-powered efficiency. Clearly, he considered himself to
be grossly overworked and under-appreciated, but in truth
he resembled not so much a company manager on the job
as a squirrel frantically zigzagging down a country road
when caught in the headlights of a car.

On this occasion he was wearing black jeans, a black and
white diagonally striped shirt and a pair of matching black
and white framed spectacles, which slid up and down his
nose with every movement of the head. Having been greeted
as warmly as one who had arrived in a well victualled yacht
at his desert island, I asked if he was the sole inhabitant of
these parts and he replied: 'Oh, Marty's somewhere around,
I believe, prowling through those underground caverns
they've got here. He's the only one of our lot, though, apart
from our revered director, who's been putting poor me
through every hoop that man can devise. We came over
together last week. How was your trip?'

'Not bad. Got in about two hours ago. Rose was on my
plane and I saw Catherine for a minute. Any news of Gilbert?'

'Yes, he's staying with some swanky millionaires in
Connecticut, or one of those. He'll be flying down in His or
Her gold-plated helicopter, wouldn't you know? Rumour
has it he'll be here tomorrow. I must say I can wait. Like to
see the latest photos of the house?'

'Not just now,' I said hastily, for Terry could be a real drag about this old barn in Provence, which he and his friend, Jocelyn, who worked in the B.B.C., were converting into an Englishman's paradise and furthermore he was not at all a gifted photographer. I had seen scores of snapshots of the dreary place at various stages of its progress and it still looked like a nasty old barn at the far end of a slightly tilted meadow.

'When I can give them my full attention,' I explained, 'I'd simply love to, but I've got a taxi outside and ten minutes is my limit. Would it be all right to take a sneak at the dressing rooms?'

'Feel free, darling!' he said, instantly losing interest in me. 'Excuse me if I don't accompany you. There'll be hell to pay if these schedules aren't finished by the time Andy gets back. All you have to do is go through that next room and you'll see the lifts. Press the one marked L.L., which means basement to you and me, and when the doors slide back the dressing rooms will be facing you. You're in number three. Your name's already up.'

I followed these directions and found that number three was opposite the middle lift and that the journey down had taken no more than five seconds. I tried the door, but it was locked, which was typical of Terry, and was debating whether to go back and ask him for the key when I heard a distant crashing noise, as of one playing about with machinery and, assuming it to have been made by the dedicated Marty, sorting out some lighting equipment, decided to go and say hallo to him instead.

The search took me past two more dressing rooms, after which there was a right angled turn into a second and similar corridor, also containing about a dozen rooms, with red arrows down the walls, indicating that the fire escape, canteen, plus a further set of elevators and sundry other amenities lay ahead. There were swing doors at the end of this passage and they led into a vast concrete cave, about fifty yards square and seeming even larger and more desolate from being practically empty. There were some wooden crates and iron pipes stacked against one of the walls and, on my right, some more boxes and half-a-dozen dummy figures clothed in realistic looking chain mail. I guessed that I was now standing directly beneath the opera stage and that these were the costumes for a recent or forthcoming production.

There was no sign of Marty, or whoever had been making the noise and there was a dank, slightly sinister atmosphere about the place, so that I was about to turn and scurry back to bright lights and carpeted floors when I heard another sound and, to my utter amazement, distinctly saw a movement on the part of one of the armour clad dummies.

In retrospect, I am almost certain that amazement and not fear was the first reaction, for by that time I had journeyed so far, in spirit as well as distance, from all the fond, familiar things that normal reflexes had become blunted and I had reached a stage of bemused acceptance, quite as powerful as if the escalator at Dulles Airport had actually been a rabbit hole. Moreover, a stranger encased in a suit of armour presents fewer hazards than the average rapist and murderer and I had advanced a few steps towards this strange phenomenon, when a pair of human hands, which had been concealed behind its back, engaged in a brief struggle to remove the headpiece and reveal the flushed and sheepish face of Hugo Dunstan.

'Hugo, my God!' I yelped, retreating again, for amazement had now given way to disbelief and, strangely enough, faint stirrings of fear as well. 'How strange to find you here, dressed like that! What can it mean?'

'Surprise, surprise, eh?' he said, laughing self-consciously and at the same time extricating himself like a self-propelling sardine from its tin, 'Cor luvaduck, I shouldn't want to be stuck in one of those jobs for long. What happens when you get an itch? Bet you never thought of that?'

I acknowledged the truth of this and he went on: 'Very quickly becomes a fixation, I can tell you. Could turn out nasty. Well, how are you, Tessa, How's tricks?'

'That's my line, isn't it? I presume this was some kind of rehearsal for one?'

'Dead right, old lady,' he said, taking my arm and steering me firmly towards the exit, 'thought it might be a lark to stand in the wings one night, dressed up in one of those family sized saucepans. Give you all a bit of a turn, what? Still, fall rather flat now, I suppose, once the word gets round, as I've no doubt it will, with you in charge.'

'Right!' I told him, 'and I should think they'll all be deeply grateful to me for nipping that little scheme in the bud. What brought you down here, anyway?'

'On the tip of my tongue to ask you the same. As for me, I was just having a snoop round, don't you know? Getting the feel of the place and all that lark. I stumbled on those costumes and got the bright idea.'

'Incidentally, Hugo, doesn't it strike you that the whole place is singularly deserted? I'd expected to find all sorts of things going on at this time of day, but apart from Terry and yourself I haven't seen a cat.'

'Because it's Monday, that's why. No performances. What they call dark. We're going to have to work on Sunday nights instead, don't forget.'

'Oh yes, of course. All one to me, though, providing we get Monday off.'

'Rather cuts into the weekend, though; not to mention the Saturday night hangover. Might as well be working on the flipping Continent.'

Terry flapped a languid hand at us, saying: 'Your taxi driver is getting a mite anxious, dear.'

'Is he? How do you know?'

'Came wandering in here looking for you. Gave me quite a turn, actually. First time I've seen a black man with red hair, I thought to myself. Don't worry, darling, I spoke up for you. Honest as the day is long, I told him and he toddled off quite happily.'

It had taken about two seconds for the miraculous truth to dawn on Hugo and as we emerged on to the marble paved passage along the side of the theatre the familiar shrewd look came into his eyes and he said with very forced humour:

'Aren't some people clever, though? I wish I'd thought of keeping my taxi simmering on the hob, but it didn't occur to me that I could get away with it. Probably wouldn't have either, not being a young and beautiful female.'

'Never mind,' I told him. 'You'll soon pick one up here. People must be rolling up non-stop for tickets to see you perform.'

'Not on a Monday they won't. Told you that already, didn't I? Everything's shut down. I suppose you couldn't be a saint and drop me off?'

'Depends which way you're going,' I said, a ruse which might have defeated lesser scroungers, but which Hugo was quite equal to.

'No, no, I wouldn't dream of taking you out of your way. Just let me know where you're bound for and I'll tell you where to drop me off.'

'Georgetown.'

'Aha! Made to measure! Me likewise! I'll crawl in first, shall I? Save you having to shovel across. Be a lamb and tell him to stop first at the Amsterdam, will you?'

Perhaps the taxi driver was not a professional at all, but merely standing in for a friend, or perhaps Hugo, who was a dab hand at sizing up the prospects, had been correct in implying that in this city young females got more co-operation than their elders, even those as beautiful and authoritative as Catherine, for once again no objections were raised about the change of route and Hugo was able to relax in his seat and congratulate himself on having saved at least two dollars.

He was even moved to pat my hand and tell me what an improvement it had made to have me in the company, no doubt under the impression that this flattery would oil the wheels for a free ride home after every performance. However, I made a silent promise to defeat this object just as soon as the jet lag had worn off.

2

A quarter of a mile to the north of Kennedy Center, at Washington Circle, there is a circular grass mound, coloured a dirty straw colour after the long hot summer, with an equestrian statue in the middle of it, where a dozen streets and avenues converge, the principal one being Pennsylvania Avenue. The bronze horse and rider are gazing reverently down the avenue towards the White House, roughly eight blocks away in a dead straight line, and have their backs turned to Georgetown.

From there it was only a five minute drive to the heart of Georgetown, where M Street crosses Wisconsin Avenue at the start of its long upward trail, cutting first through the skein of eighteenth-century streets and lanes, past the woods and glens which border Massachusetts Avenue and finally levelling out into the endlessly repetitive Maryland suburbs.

Lorraine's house was tucked away some hundred yards from the main road on the first stage of this journey and not very far from Hugo's hotel, although I was obliged to waste another two or three minutes while he raked through his nasty little plastic purse in a fruitless attempt to find the right change for his share and then to listen to him swearing on cub's honour to settle up next time we met.

There was a short flight of steps leading up to the little brick and timber house called 1312A, which was perched eight or ten feet above street level, and on every second step a stone urn containing straggly, dejected looking petunias and geraniums. The second urn from the top was my objective and, following instructions, I tilted it to one side and groped underneath, experiencing yet another plunge of the spirits when my fingers came in contact with a key. However, before I could straighten up again and steel myself to enter a strange and deserted house, the door was flung open and Lorraine appeared on the stoop, like a ray of sunshine lighting up a hostile world.

'Saw you from my bedroom window,' she called. 'I'd almost given you up, or thought I had the wrong date. Where've you been all this time? I phoned the airport and they told me the plane landed hours ago.'

'I know, Lorraine, it's a long story.'

'Save it till later, then. Just come on in and put those bags down. You can leave the key where it was. That's its home. Saves a whole lot of bother.'

'What about the drug sodden rapists and murderers?' I asked feebly, a mild hysteria having resulted from my relief at seeing her. 'Aren't you worried?'

'No, they have their own, we don't have to bother about them. Come on in, I have a million things to tell you.'

I obeyed, although almost eight hours passed before I heard one of them and by then it was getting on for midnight. When we had manoeuvred ourselves and the luggage past a bicycle parked in the tiny hall, antipollution and energy conservation being two of Lorraine's current patriotic obsessions, and were seated in her cosy, untidy living room, half of whose space was filled by a grand piano, she offered me a drink which I declined on the somewhat irrelevant grounds that I had no idea what time it was. This prompted her to subject me to a more searching scrutiny, whereupon she instantly jumped up again and commanded me to go straight upstairs to bed, using more or less the same formula as Catherine's and adding that she was not about to waste the valuable, highly sought after story of her life on a jet laggard who had no business crawling around in a state of semi-coma and that she would use the interval to work on a Chopin Étude, having promised herself to master all twenty-four of them before her fiftieth birthday.

CHAPTER FOUR

LORRAINE at this time was in her late thirties, tall, dark and starry eyed and beginning to put on weight. However, this did not matter at all, since neither her charm nor popularity depended on her looks and, as she was pure gold from the top of her cropped, untidy head to the tips of her sloppy sandals, it was rather a question of the more of her the better.

It came as no surprise at all that nine hundred thousand of the million things she had to tell me concerned her latest divorce and her newest love. She had already been married four times, for, in addition to being pure gold, she was extremely moral and would not have contemplated entering into an informal relationship with someone she was deeply in love with, if he were free to marry her. I think this may be true of many Americans, men as well as women, and sometimes gives rise to misunderstandings abroad.

Unfortunately, she was invariably unlucky in love and it was typical of her case history that the only one of her husbands who had been rich, faithful and kind hearted, should have been killed in an aeroplane crash eighteen months after they were married. She did not even profit financially because, although as a result of his death she had inherited the house in Washington, as well as a posh apartment on Park Avenue and a little shack in California, this husband had also been married before and was the father of several children. Under the terms of his will, while debarred from selling any of these properties, she received an income which was totally inadequate for their proper maintenance and, as a result, was chronically, often embarrassingly hard up. In the intervals between subsequent marriages, she had made spirited efforts to earn a living and occasionally to acquire some qualifications to this end and was currently employed by the Smithsonian Institution, in what capacity I never quite gathered, although it must have been on a part-time basis, or perhaps in liaison with some other museum, for it enabled her to make frequent, sometimes prolonged trips to New York.

An earlier venture had been her enrolment at a drama school, followed by a brief but moderately successful career on the stage. I had always assumed that the reason for this coming to an abrupt end was that the unsocial hours had conflicted with affairs of the heart, but on that first evening of my stay in Georgetown, as we chatted our way into the small hours, some stray remark of mine concerning Toby's play set her off in reminiscence and I heard the true reason why, with the ball roughly speaking at her feet, she had so mysteriously faded from the theatrical scene.

It was some disparaging reference to Gilbert Mann which set her going and she began by saying:

'So no illusions there, Tessa? Boy, am I glad to hear that?'

'Why glad?'

'Oh well, you know, he does have this charisma, or whatever, and a lot of people never do see beyond it. Even when the carpet's been pulled from under so fast that they crack their skulls going down, they still come back for more. I've seen that more times than I can count and I was scared out of my mind it might happen to you.'

'I'd have put you out of your misery ages ago if I'd known how it weighed on you, but I wasn't aware that you even knew him.'

'Well, it's true that I might not even recognise him now, if I passed him on the street; except I suppose I'd know that arrogant walk anywhere, and I'll bet that hasn't changed.'

'But you knew him well at one time? In your shady past?'

'Oh sure, none better. We were in a play together at the Music Box, when he was the great ascending star and everyone's romantic hero and I was making my first and only appearance on Broadway. I was all set to reach the heights in those days too, and I thought I had it made when the reviews came out. It was quite a while before the truth hit me and I realised that, so far as my career was concerned, it was downhill all the way from then on.'

'Implying that Gilbert was to blame?'

'Not just implying, Buster; saying it right out, loud and clear, in four languages. Mind you, there was a little bad luck mixed up in it and some mind blowing stupidity on my part, but it was Gilbert with his little axe who did all the hard work.'

'Was he jealous of your notices, or . . . or perhaps you don't want to talk about it?'

'Sure I do, I love to talk about it. There was a time when . . . but this is going back nearly twenty years, for God's sake, and you can't keep bearing the same grudge for ever. It just occasionally hits me to this day when I go to see some play and there's an actress, about my age, who gets a big hand for her first entrance, but maybe didn't start out with any more talent than I had, and I get to thinking what I could do with the salary she's raking in now . . . well, you know how it is, Tessa? But it's mainly on account of someone like yourself, who's just starting out, that I get really jumpy.'

'I've had no brushes with him so far, if that's any comfort to you. Don't imagine that we're equals or anything, but he's very cordial, in a patronising kind of way.'

'No comfort at all, you have to believe me, Tessa. All during rehearsals and the first few weeks of the run, I'd have said exactly the same about him myself, but that doesn't amount to a thing where Gilbert's concerned. It's the stab in the back you have to watch out for.'

'Which you got? Why and what happened?' I asked again.

'Well, first I got sick. No, I admit that was no fault of Gilbert's and I wasn't pregnant either, if that's what you're thinking. It was a complaint they call trigeminal neuralgia. There's a nerve somewhere around the base of the ear and it gets inflamed or whatever and starts slashing your face with invisible knives. At least, that's the best way I can describe it and it's something I wouldn't wish on my worst enemy. It still comes back once in a while, but there are drugs now which control it, so it's not the same problem. In those days you had to get by with ordinary painkillers, which were about as effective as a slug of brandy to a man having his leg amputated. Anyway, it got so terrible that I couldn't even remember my lines, let alone open my mouth wide enough to be heard in the front row, so I had to leave the play for a while. I wasn't badly worried. The understudy took over and wasn't all that hot, and the doctor told me it could last several weeks, but would more likely clear up in just a few days. I guess I'm naturally optimistic and I was so darn sure that I could lick it if I really concentrated that I never seriously considered any other alternative. And that's exactly how it was. After three days resting up and rolling my head in scarves even to go to the bathroom, I was so much better that I was able to get back to the theatre and sign on again. Did you say something?'

'Not really. I was just wondering about Gilbert's part in all this, but I suppose you're coming to it. Sorry to interrupt.'

'There isn't much more. I went back, beaming all over my silly face and expecting just about everyone except the understudy to fling their arms around my neck and got the kind of backhander which made all the rest seem like a picnic in June.'

'How was that?'

'I'd been fired. They told me they were getting someone in to replace me, had already engaged her, in fact. They tore my contract into little pieces and threw them in my face.'

'But, Lorraine, how could that be? Being ill doesn't count as breach of contract. I don't understand.'

'Me neither, until they spelt it out for me, but it was true all right.'

'But they can't sack someone for being off sick for a few days.'

'That's right, they can't; not unless Gilbert Mann happens to be around to show them how. You know what?'

'No.'

'He'd conned the management into accepting there was nothing wrong with me except my own vices. In words of one syllable, I was an alcoholic and liable to disappear on a bender, or pass out cold in the second act, any time at all.

If you study the small print you'll find that's one ground where they can legally fire you.'

'I know that, but it still doesn't make sense. Why would they take Gilbert's word against yours in a case of that sort? There must have been medical evidence to back you up, for a start?'

'Oh, sure, and my doctor came up with all the right reports, but everyone knows it's not too difficult to fake that kind of evidence and furthermore this is one of those complaints which don't produce any visible symptoms. It doesn't show up in the blood tests or X-rays. It's just a nagging old nerve, no convenient swollen glands, or nice disfiguring rash. And there was something else to add to his credibility.'

'Oh dear!'

'Partly that wasn't any of my fault either, partly, I have to admit, my own crass stupidity was to blame. Plenty of witnesses too, since I hadn't seen any reason for concealment.'

'What are you on about now?'

'Well, first, like I told you, I had this pain all over one half of my face and it affected my speech. I was like someone who'd had a minor stroke, I guess, and the words came out kind of slurred and indistinct. What didn't occur to me in my beautiful innocence, and thinking what a brave little old trouper I was to go on at all, was they also came out like someone who'd swigged half a bottle of neat scotch. You can imagine how Gilbert capitalised on that?'

'Though it's hard to believe anyone could be so rotten. What about the other, the thing you were partly to blame for?'

'Ah! That was just the miserable fact that on one occasion, in full view of half-a-dozen articulate witnesses, I did put down quite a quantity of neat scotch. Not half a bottle, but more than I was used to and more than I could handle. I got this crazy notion that a strong shot of alcohol might help numb the pain and also give me the confidence to get through. I was so desperate by that time I was ready to try even a fool idea like that. Naturally, it didn't work. I gave an even worse performance that night and that's when I gave in; but by then Gilbert had all the ammunition he needed.'

'But it was still based on a fallacy and I still don't understand how he got away with it. You should have fought back, Lorraine; sued for wrongful dismissal, or slander even.'

'Oh, I did all that, don't worry! There wasn't a single idiot thing I left undone. I sued for the lot and that was where I made my biggest mistake of all.'

'Why?'

'Because if I'd bowed out gracefully it would all have been forgotten in a few weeks. No one outside our own small circle would have known much about it and it wouldn't have lasted there, once a fresh scandal came along. I could have lived it down and that's what I should have done, but instead it dragged on for months, with all the worst kind of publicity and by the time I was through there wasn't a soul in the business who hadn't heard the lurid details, and you know that saying about smoke without fire? I wasn't a big enough name to survive it and by the time the story was forgotten I was good and forgotten too. Well, you know, yourself, how it is Tessa? If there's a choice between two available actresses and one of them doesn't have the reputation of hitting the bottle and suing the management, she's the one they pick.'

This was true, but I also knew a little about persecution complexes, which seem to be rampant among out-of-work actors and although I had no doubt that Lorraine was sincere in all she had told me, I still believed she might be deluding herself to some extent. Phrasing these reservations as tactfully as I could, I said: 'On the other hand, perhaps it wouldn't have made all that much difference? What I mean is, if Gilbert was really gunning for you he'd have struck again the minute you were back on your feet. I don't know what you'd done to get your name in his little black book, but from what some of his other victims have told me, it wouldn't have been ticked off that easily. When he gets the knife in he leaves it there and keeps on turning.'

'I was never in his black book,' Lorraine said impatiently, getting up to throw another log on the fire. 'There was nothing personal in this. I thought I'd made that clear.'

'Not to me.'

'Well, maybe I didn't see any need to. What would he have to fear from me, for God's sake? A little, obscure fledgling, way down on the billing and practically sweeping the carpet with my forehead every time the big star came by? No, there was nothing personal in it, I just happened to be in his way. A pawn in the game is what I was.'

'What game?'

'The one certain gentlemen play when they mix business with bed. He'd fallen for some dancer who had yearnings to go legitimate. He was there to see that she did and they both thought my part would be just right for her. Hadn't I mentioned that?'

'No.'

'Well, you know me. I don't have the British phlegm or whatever. Once I get steamed up it all comes out as I think of it, which means next to incomprehensible. That's how it was, though.'

'What was this girl's name?'

'Deirdre Molton, as though I could ever forget! I'm about the only one who hasn't, however. She didn't last too long.'

'It rings a bell, though. Didn't he marry her at one point?'

'Yes, she was his number three and they stayed married for all of fifteen months. I guess there've been several more since her. Deirdre took an overdose when he moved on to number four, which must have saved him a whole lot of bother. So I suppose I didn't come off too badly. Probably the real thing to watch for with Gilbert is not so much the black book as the lecherous gleam. Anyway, you haven't fallen into either category, thank the Lord, so there's no problem there and my own story was over years ago; long enough, anyway, to have acquired a sense of proportion about it. My life would certainly have been different if Gilbert hadn't taken a hand in it, but it doesn't necessarily follow that it would have been that much better.'

This was certainly a sensible attitude and I would have given a lot to believe in it, but Lorraine was a woman ruled by her emotions, if ever I knew one, and there had been a jerkiness in her movements and a most uncharacteristic hardening of the mouth when she was relating her unhappy experience, which suggested that it still caused her pain in recollection. It was enough to change my mind about inviting her along to the theatre one morning, to meet Toby and maybe sit in at a rehearsal. With a caution which I recognised as unutterably despicable, I told myself that an encounter between her and Gilbert could be embarrassing for both of them and might, through association, prove damaging to my own prospects as well.

CHAPTER FIVE

1

I WAS awakened just before ten the next morning by a cheerful female of massive proportions, who introduced herself as Muriel, the cleaning lady. Her radiant humour and refreshing literal mindedness were to be a source of great comfort in the trials ahead and she got off to a rattling start by presenting me with a breakfast tray which included half a pint of orange juice and half a gallon of piping hot coffee, as well as a copy of the *Washington Post*, which was constructed on equally lavish lines, consisting of approximately one hundred pages, of which ninety-two were devoted to advertising.

Besides being friendly and good natured, Muriel was very loquacious and, having deposited her bounty, launched into a dramatic account of a shooting affray which had occurred in her street the previous night and in which, as she had afterwards learnt from neighbours, two men had been killed outright and a third left bleeding to death on the sidewalk. I asked her if this kind of thing happened often and she replied that it did. She then surprised me even more by showing a keen interest in Scotland, questioning me closely on the subject, as though anxious to reassure herself that it still existed, and it transpired that about twenty years before she had gone to Glasgow on a package tour with her Church group and, most surprising of all, had enjoyed every minute.

It soon became obvious that she would not readily run out of interesting topics for discussion, although dusting and straightening up my bedroom the whole time she was talking, so I explained that I had to get up and bath and dress myself with some speed, having promised to meet my cousin Toby, who was due in from New York at midday.

Muriel then asked me if Toby was a Scotch name, so I agreed that it was and she went away looking highly delighted.

I had sidestepped the truth by a centimetre in implying that I intended to meet Toby at his point of arrival in Washington, although this had been my intention until I learned that he was travelling down by train. The journey by air from New York takes approximately forty minutes and the planes come into National Airport, which is only a ten minute drive from the city centre, but practicalities of that nature had never been known to influence Toby, whose distrust of all forms of mechanical transport functioned in direct ratio to their speed and efficiency and he would doubtless have made the trip by covered wagon, if one had been available. The train was certainly the next worst thing, for it takes six times as long as the aeroplane, is invariably late and pulls into a station which is itself about half-way to Baltimore.

In view of this I had decided to let him stew in his own diesel and had arranged to meet him for dinner at his hotel, which was the Watergate. In the meantime, this being my last free day before the rehearsal schedule clamped down, it was my intention to explore the city on my own.

I was squeezing past the bicycle on my way to the front door when the telephone rang and I halted, as is my custom on such occasions, being curious to know who was calling, even in the unlikelihood of its being any of my business. Muriel came ambling in from the kitchen to answer it and after a few 'yeahs' and 'uh huhs', she flapped her hand at me in a detaining, though patently superfluous manner.

'There's a Mr Dunstan wants to talk to you,' she announced, beckoning me with the receiver, 'says why don't you call round at his place this morning, so you and he can look at some of the sights? You want to talk to him?'

'No, no, be an angel and say I've gone out, will you, Muriel?' I said, preparing to translate words into action with all speed, since it was no part of my programme to provide Hugo with a free conducted tour. 'Tell him I won't be back till five,' I added just before nipping out of the front door.

The last stop on my tour was the Hirschorn Museum, which is one of the most recent additions to the glories of Washington and affectionately known as the donut. In fact, it is an impressive, circular building, set in a paved courtyard, containing sculptures ancient and modern, with Henry Moore taking his usual proud place in front of the main entrance. Inside, in the devious style of department stores, the escalators are so arranged that the customer is provided with a totally different view of the exhibits on the downward journey from the one going up, which is quite a snare for the compulsive rubberneck, and I was about to re-alight on the second floor, for a closer look at some objects I had missed the first time, when I noticed something else which, after a fractional hesitation, caused me to continue my descent without a break. It was not a painting or *objet d'art* which had caught my eye, but the sight of Rose, with a look of utter, devastated doom on her face, seated side by side with Terry Rack on one of the leather couches, their heads practically touching. It was not so much tact on my part to move on before either of them noticed me, for I was aware that it would have been an act of mercy to have sailed up and released poor Rose from the torment of having to look at Terry's awful photographs, but sight-seeing takes its toll of nervous energy and I quailed at the thought of having to expend still more of it by sharing her ordeal until Catherine rescued us both.

Thus, escape was my only thought until it had been achieved, but while driving back towards Pennsylvania Avenue, as I mentally reviewed the scene, placing the invisible Catherine peering indefatigably about in some other part of the room, it struck me as a heavy coincidence that three members of the company besides myself should have turned up in that particular building at precisely the same time. However, the number could be reduced to two by fusing Catherine and Rose into a single entity, which was the natural thing to do, and furthermore the Hirschorn would come high on any visitor's list, since it was a novelty even to some who had known the city before. In this way I contrived to manufacture a small mystery for myself, only to have it solved even before the ride was over.

2

It was getting on for seven when I arrived at the Watergate Hotel, but when the reception clerk had transmitted the news to Toby's suite, he turned back to me with the request that I should wait a short while, as my party would be right down. This conjured up visions of hilarious crowds surging out of the elevators and waving balloons, but in fact when the doors slid back only Toby emerged and he did not look at all in a party mood.

'Where can we go?' he asked in his most fretful tones, 'I'd prefer it to be very, very far away, but everyone tells me that if I show my face in the streets I shall have it slashed with knives before I've gone two yards. The whole thing is such a worry.'

'I know,' I sympathised, 'I've had all that thrown at me too and I'm bored stiff with it. If you ask me, the whole story has been invented by Rose Henneky, to put the fear of God into us; and the funny thing is that I've noticed dozens of people walking about and none of them looks in the least apprehensive.'

'They're probably all thieves and slashers themselves, looking for a likely prospect. It doesn't reassure me at all. On the other hand, if we stay cowering here we are liable to run into Gilbert, which would be even more upsetting.'

'Luckily, there is a solution,' I said, 'I happen to know of a little bar tucked away ever so discreetly in the building next door and we can reach it without so much as setting foot on a public highway. It's buried among a lot of boutiques, what's more, so Gilbert would never find us.'

'Oh, very well, if you say so. I suppose that wouldn't entail any serious risk.'

'So long as we move fast and keep our heads down. Ready?'

'You do get around, don't you, Tessa?' he asked me in wondering tones a few minutes later. 'How on earth did you stumble on this one?'

The question was aptly phrased because, like so many establishments of its kind, it was not only inaccessibly situated but so dark inside that the customer was temporarily blinded and liable to collide with the mock font, filled with plastic flowers, which had been placed immediately inside the entrance. It is an odd perversity, for in general there is nothing in the service or merchandise on offer to be shame-faced about and must, I believe, reflect some deep rooted national prejudice, paralleled to some extent by certain rich people nearer home who buy the priciest car on the market, while insisting that it should be in the most hideous colour the manufacturer can devise, perhaps with the sub-conscious idea of indulging themselves to the hilt without incurring the envy of the less fortunate.

I tested this theory on Toby, who was not impressed: 'For God's sake, Tessa, no homespun philosophies today, I beg you. I'm worn to a shred, as it is, and comparisons between national mores is the second most boring subject in the world.'

'What is the first most boring?'

'Any and every one raised by Gilbert.'

Nobly resisting the temptation to deluge him with 'I told you so's', I pressed for details.

'One very boring thing is that he's nagging me to death to re-write part of his scene with Hugo. He feels that one or two of the laughs come in the wrong place and it all needs tightening up. You and I both know what he means by that.'

'Will you oblige?'

'I suppose I'll have to. It's rather rough on Hugo, having his only two funny lines cut, but one has to think of the greatest good of the greatest number.'

'So that's all right then; all smiles again?'

'Not at all. We'd hardly got that tedious, underhand business dealt with when Andy dropped in to shake my hand in welcome and Gilbert immediately started on him.'

'What about?'

'About sacking Terry.'

'Andy can't do that, he has no right to.'

'Try explaining that to Gilbert.'

'Anyway, it would be murder to have someone new brought in at this stage. What's Terry done to offend him?'

'Deserted his post, I gather. Gilbert urgently needed him to deal with some perfectly pointless, egocentric matter and Terry was not available.'

'Well, that really takes the bun! After all, he is supposed to be the company manager and he could have been out on some perfectly legitimate business.'

'Only, knowing Terry, it's more likely that he wasn't.'

'But didn't Andy invent some story to cover up for him?'

'No, on the contrary, he handled it in the silliest way imaginable. Instead of pursing his lips and promising to have Terry hung, drawn and quartered, he took your line that, with all his deficiencies, chaos would come again if we were to replace him now, even in the unlikely event of being able to get someone out from London in time.'

'Sounds reasonable to me.'

'Very reasonable and very naive.'

'In what way?'

'The great thing to remember about Gilbert, Tessa, is that he rarely makes a move without some ulterior shady motive. Anyone a fraction less starry-eyed than our trusting little director would have seen a mile off that Gilbert would hardly bother to exert himself to smash poor Terry into a thousand pieces, unless there was something in it for himself.'

'And did you find out what that was?'

'Naturally, since it was the only part of the argument which interested me. Otherwise I should have left them to it. They had both obviously forgotten it was my room they were using for a battleground, so I shouldn't have been missed. Luckily, you turned up just as the last card was thrown on the table, which was very convenient.'

'I pride myself on my timing. What did the cards reveal?'

'It was an anti-climax really, just about the oldest move in the game. Gilbert has some dear friends in Connecticut, who just happen to be multi-millionaires and, by an even stranger coincidence, with a son who majored in stage management, or some nonsense. This boy has but one ambition in life and you can probably guess what it is.'

'You mean poor old Terry is getting the push so that this other one can have his big chance?'

'In a nutshell. Gilbert is much too shrewd to have him brought in as A.S.M., or in any capacity which requires a modicum of ability, but he rightly imagines that anyone with a grain of common sense could do Terry's job on his head. When I left them he was working round to the proposition that the young man be brought in to learn the ropes, with a view to taking over when we get to New York.'

'This boy hasn't got a beautiful sister, by any chance?'

'That wouldn't surprise me, since they appear to be even more rolling in it than the last family he married into. What became of that one, by the way?'

'Daphne? She's still around, so far as I know. Someone mentioned that she'd threatened to come over for the first night, but I don't know about that. Presumably, Gilbert will head her off, if he's found richer fish to fry.'

'Well, Daphne's quite able to take care of herself and personally, I don't give a damn how he conducts his private life, so long as it doesn't interfere with business. These shoddy manoeuvres are too vulgar for words. He'll get himself disliked if he doesn't take a pull.'

'It's like one of those trad detective stories, don't you think, Toby? You know, where there's one character who's loathed and feared by about half-a-dozen others and when he gets knocked off they all start lying like mad and you have to guess which one is guilty.'

'You think this will happen to Gilbert? That's good news!'

'I wouldn't depend on it, but I do know that whoever I'm talking to nowadays, the anti-Gilbert motif crops up sooner or later. It's building up into the classic pattern and I've been trying to work out in advance who would be the most likely to crack his skull. Not either of us, naturally, that goes without saying.'

'I can't promise that it goes the whole way without saying, in my case.'

'Yes, you can, because it wouldn't be playing fair with the reader.'

'Indeed? Well, I suppose it's a relief, in a way. Who did you consider the most promising?'

'Well, Hugo wouldn't do badly,' I said, 'though perhaps a shade too obvious. We might have him in as a red herring, nursing a very loudly expressed grievance about having his part slashed to ribbons. Then there's Terry, who's about to lose his job, which I know for a fact will be a dreadful worry for him and probably put back the conversion work on his barn to a catastrophic degree.'

'Yes, I like that one,' Toby agreed, 'I always find financial motives the most convincing of all. Anyone else?'

'There's Andy. This will be the first play ever that he's directed on Broadway. The chances of success will be seriously diminished if Gilbert reduces the entire cast to a state of screaming jitters, so we've got the financial aspect there, not to mention Andy's reputation.'

'I'm afraid that's rather weak, you know, Tessa. I've known productions where the whole company was split down the middle, with no one on either side speaking to anyone on the other, and they've run for years and years.'

'Maybe so, but the average reader wouldn't be so ready to believe that and you'll have no call to refer to it when you give your evidence to the police.'

'Oh, shall we have to do that? Couldn't they send for Robin to straighten it out? No, I suppose that wouldn't appeal. Anyone else on your list?'

'Catherine's next,' I told him, tapping my fourth finger, 'I haven't thoroughly worked out her motive yet, but there's enough animosity floating around in that quarter to make it worth a try. Though, I think if we're going to include her, we'd better make it death by poisoning. She's getting a little too frail for the blunt instrument and firearms wouldn't be in her line either. Too noisy. Strychnine in the prop whisky might be the answer. Quite a neat method and readily available to one and all.'

'Right. So now we know the method and we have four suspects. Would that be enough?'

'Five really, because if Catherine is there we can certainly throw Rose in as well. She hasn't any personal quarrel with Gilbert, as far as I know, but it could always be said that she was protecting Catherine.'

'What could it always be said that she was protecting her from?'

'Oh, any old thing. That will emerge as we go along.'

'Except that I see a snag here. It's Catherine who is the great protector in that relationship. It needs a little more working out, if you want a frank criticism. And you'd be wasting your time, unfortunately,' he added after a short pause, 'it's an attractive idea, but built on sand. Financially and in other ways too, there isn't one of these people, with the possible exception of Terry, who wouldn't be a lot worse off with Gilbert dead than with Gilbert alive.'

'Yes,' I admitted, 'that is the true snag, and perhaps it is all for the best. Our lives are complicated enough just now, without having sudden death thrown in. Besides, police investigations in this country might not be quite as cosy as the kind we're used to. Never mind, these fantasies are good for morale. They sublimate the aggressions and you'll probably have a much happier relationship with Gilbert in future.'

'I believe you are right,' Toby said, sounding a little surprised about it, 'I fancy that from now on I shall never quite rid myself of the belief that his life has but a short while to run, and that is bound to arouse my compassion.'

CHAPTER SIX

BY A curious coincidence, it shortly began to look as though Gilbert, too, had received intimations of mortality and was dedicating his remaining days to creating happy memories for posterity.

A rehearsal session had been called for ten a.m. and most of it was spent in accustoming ourselves to our new surroundings. The auditorium seated about three times the number of the average London theatre, presenting formidable acoustical problems for the less experienced among us, and the stage too was like a gymnasium compared to those we had been brought up on. Our designer had sought to overcome this obstacle with the use of drapes to construct a stage within a stage, but this in turn created unexpected technical difficulties, with the result that by the end of the morning nerves were growing ragged and a heavy depression had set in.

The shining exception was Gilbert who, whatever his private feelings, managed to conceal them behind a sunny mask, which remained uncracked to the end. In the circumstances, even a mild display of temperament on his part would have acted like a lighted match on gunpowder, but for once the match was not struck.

We broke at twelve-thirty because he was engaged to take part in a live radio chat show, to be broadcast from the restaurant on the top floor. The rest of us lunched off sandwiches which Terry had had sent in, and it was lucky that Gilbert escaped this particular ordeal, for they were repellent enough to put his good humour to the acid test. It was to be hoped that Gilbert's protégé would at least serve up something more appetising when his turn came, although I noticed that Terry himself seemed perfectly at one with the world, so perhaps after all Andy had won that particular battle, or perhaps Terry was still unaware that the battle was on. Andy's own demeanour might have provided a clue about this, but unfortunately he was not on view, he and Catherine and Rose having retired to eat their lunch in Catherine's dressing room, where I strongly suspected the sandwiches had been dumped in the waste paper basket and they were all tucking into selections from the Fuller refrigerator.

Hugo was loudest of all in his complaints about our soggy sandwiches and invited each of us in turn to join him in a beer in the roof cafeteria. We all knew what that meant and each in turn declined, so in the end he accepted his destiny and went off alone. We hardly took in this unusual display of resignation, however, because his departure was almost immediately followed by shrieks from Terry, who was rampaging through the drawers of his desk, tossing papers and files around in all directions.

'I'm being a bore, I know,' he said tearfully, in response to our irritable enquiries, 'and I do realise so well that it hasn't the slightest importance to anyone but myself, but I've been taking these photographs at every stage of the conversions and now there's a whole batch of them missing. I was just going to get them out to show off a bit to Jackie and Clive and they're not flipping well here. I know I had them yesterday too.'

'Haven't you kept the negatives?' I asked, trying to rustle up a little concern.

'Oh, I expect so, but not with me. They're in London, as it happens, but that's not the point. The point is that they were here, in this drawer, I know it for a fact, and now they've gone. Somebody must have pinched them, that's all I can think.'

'I don't know who would want to do that,' I said, speaking, I felt sure, for us all, 'it's much more likely that you'll find them at your hotel.'

Maddened by this palpable indifference to his misfortune, Terry's complaints became more fretful than ever and only the arrival of Andy, to remind us to be on stage in five minutes, brought the business to an end.

I was the first to go down and when I stepped out of the lift Catherine's door was closed. However, two minutes later, when I emerged from my own room, it was wide open and, not resisting the temptation to take a peek inside, I saw Rose lying flat on her back on the couch, her thin legs stretched out straight and a white compress covering the upper half of her face, producing a singularly macabre effect, as of a stone effigy on a Crusader's tomb.

Catherine was standing by her dressing table, holding a pair of spectacles in one hand and in the other a huge Italian straw basket, which accompanied her everywhere and contained, besides her copy of the script, an assortment of knitting and books, throat lozenges and letters and writing paper, as well as a mass of other impedimenta to see her through the day.

She had evidently been on the point of leaving and had then turned back to retrieve the glasses and, when she glanced up and saw me, a rather terrifying expression of displeasure darkened her features. However, to my relief, it passed instantly and, holding the glasses against her mouth, she came towards me, moving with exaggerated, tip toeing caution. There was no suggestion of dismissal in this and I waited until she joined me in the passage and had gently closed the door behind her.

'Poor Rose is sleeping at last,' she explained in a low voice, 'and woe betide anyone who wakes her!'

'What is it?' I asked. 'Another migraine?'

'So it would seem, but the worst I ever remember, and the pills hardly seem to have any effect at all.'

'When did it start?'

'Yesterday evening. Neither of us slept a wink. Did you press the right button, dear? I don't detect any sound of movement behind those walls.'

'It's coming now,' I assured her, as the red light went out.

'If only one knew of some really trustworthy doctor,' Catherine continued, preceding me into the lift. 'I've seen several brass plates in our neighbourhood, but most of them have the most peculiar names and it rather puts one off.'

'Perhaps American doctors tend to come from peculiar places. Someone must have a list, though, haven't they? I assume that one or two have been assigned to us, in case of emergencies.'

'No doubt, but that wasn't quite what I had in mind. I'd rather have someone who'd been personally recommended.'

'In that case, Miss Fuller, would you allow me to ask my friend, Lorraine? She knows absolutely everyone in Washington, including lots of posh doctors, even though she can't afford their fees herself.'

Catherine had been walking ahead of me towards the stage, but she stopped in the wings to turn and lay a hand on my arm, switching on the radiant smile which made slaves of us all:

'How very kind and thoughtful of you, Tessa! And how stupid of me not to have asked you before!'

'I'll see to it immediately after rehearsal,' I assured her in a breathless gabble. 'Don't worry, Miss Fuller, she's bound to know someone who specialises in that kind of illness.'

I was rewarded with a carbon copy of the smile, fainter and more abstracted this time and then she turned her back on me and I knew that I had ceased to exist for her when I saw her shoulders straighten and her head thrown back, ready for her entrance on stage.

Even in my bemused glow it struck me as strange and a little pathetic that she should bother to go through this routine for a perfectly ordinary rehearsal, with not a photographer or reporter in sight. It could have been simple force of habit, but there was also the possibility that her anxiety was deeper than she had let on and that these gestures reflected a conscious effort to throw off her worries and immerse herself in the job. This was partly true, as it happened, although there was a good deal more to it than that.

CHAPTER SEVEN

WHETHER she was aware of it or not, and I suspect that she was, Catherine stood in relation to the younger members of the company as an admired but intimidating headmistress. Such was her charm and authority that we tumbled over each other to dance attendance and, as soon as there was a break in rehearsal, I went into Terry's office to telephone Lorraine and request her to busy herself in the matter of finding the most brilliant and polished migraine specialist the city had to offer. I had gambled on having the room to myself, for obviously it was preferable to talk in private and, up to a point, the gamble paid off. Terry was not there and my guess that as soon as the coast was clear he would nip over to his hotel to look for his precious photographs was probably correct. However, luck ran out there because there was no reply from Lorraine's number. I allowed the ringing to continue for some while, just in case it was having to compete with a Chopin Étude, but was finally obliged to hang up when Andy arrived, looking very moody blues and irritable.

'Seen Terry?' he asked.

'He's not here at the moment.'

'That I can tell, and when is he ever, blast his boots!'

'He could be out on some task or other; or conferring with the front of the house people.'

'Then he should bloody well have told me about it. Things are dicey enough without this kind of inefficiency. You'd think at least the office could run smoothly, whatever else.'

'Why so distraught? Not another crisis?'

'You could say that. You've just missed a charming little scene where Gilbert had Jackie in tears for the second time today. If he pushes her around much more I have a feeling we'll be in real trouble. Clive would probably have gone for him with fisticuffs if Hugo hadn't intervened. He practically held Clive back by force, our brave little Biggles. And even Catherine looks ready to drop, which tells you what Gilbert can do when he really puts his mind to it.'

'I don't think she had much sleep last night, but what beats me, Andy, is what Gilbert gains by upsetting everyone. You can't really tell me that there's any advantage to him in reducing us all to the miserable jitters?'

'As I understand it, he can't really help himself. It's partly a matter of temperament. Underneath all the swagger he's dead nervous, you know, and it's worse than ever now because he really has got something to be nervous about.'

'What?'

'Acoustics. He literally hasn't got the voice for a theatre of this size and he knows it. He sailed through this morning because his mind was mainly on this broadcast he was doing, but it's hit him now, to the point where he can no longer kid himself that he'll be okay when he really works on it. It's a tough one because his whole style is based on the barely audible throwaway and the totally inaudible throwaway won't have quite the same impact. I want to see what can be done with a few discreet mikes and I need Terry to stand by and help me organise it. If you should see him, warn him to stay put, for God's sake, but don't tell him why. I don't want the word to get around.'

'I should think not,' I said haughtily, 'microphones, indeed! Whatever next?'

'I have no idea what next,' he replied wearily, 'all I do know is that whether we like it or not something has to be done. I can just see the notices if we open as we are now and that certainly won't make Gilbert any easier to live with. Also, this may be news to you, but American companies often use mikes.'

'Which won't cut much ice with Miss Fuller. You can guess what her reaction will be, can't you?'

'Yes, thank you, but I'll take one crisis at a time, if you've no objection. We'll cross that bridge when we've blown up this one.'

'Or you could try pushing Gilbert under a bus before any more rot sets in? How about that?'

'Don't tempt me!' Andy begged. 'And don't forget, love, if you should see Terry—'

Curiously enough, I did see him, although not until after the working day was over, by which time I had made another futile attempt to telephone Lorraine and everyone, including Andy, had left the theatre. It was about six o'clock, a still, pink and orange evening, with the sun descending majestically behind Mount Vernon and the traffic thickening up for the long, winding trail to suburban homes. Georgetown and points beyond are among the most popular destinations for the commuting population and, apart from the hopelessness of finding an empty taxi, I decided that it would be as quick, as well as more agreeable on such an evening, to make the journey on foot.

Terry and I practically collided at Washington Circle, both of us with our eyes riveted on the traffic signals as we waited to cross one of the innumerable streets which converge there.

'Walk, Don't Walk, Don't Walk, Fall Over, Get Up,' he muttered angrily, recognising me a split second before our next instructions sent us both plunging across to another section of No Man's Land. 'It drives you mad after a bit! Makes you feel like a zombie, or something.'

'You'll be feeling worse still if you don't walk in Andy's direction pretty smartly. Patience is running low in that quarter. Where the hell did you get to, if you'll forgive my asking?'

'Well, there's these . . . figures I needed and I'd left them in my hotel room. It's over on H Street and I've had to walk the whole way back. What am I supposed to do, anyway? He gets livid if he's interrupted during rehearsal and I can't be everywhere at once, can I?'

'It's more a question of the right place at the right time. I speak as a friend,' I told him.

'Oh, no offence, but if I hadn't been able to produce these figures there'd have been hell to pay on that account. Thanks for tipping me off, though. I'd better Walk and Don't Walk my way back to the theatre and pour some honey all over him.'

'Too late for that now, Terry. I'd try his hotel, if I were you.'

'Oh, blimey, I can't even remember where he's staying. Somewhere in Georgetown, I do know, but that would hardly suffice, I suppose. I'll have to go back and look him up on the list. Honestly, what a life! And I was hoping to get to a movie this evening.'

'You may yet, because I know his address. He's at the Amsterdam. I've heard Hugo trying to cadge a lift off him.'

'Oh, bless you, ducks. That'll save a bit of time, not to mention my bacon.'

'And I've learnt a marvellous route from my friend, Lorraine, where I'm staying. It takes us through all the back doubles and brings us out slap by the Amsterdam.'

Nevertheless, he insisted on accompanying me the whole way to Lorraine's and wasted a few more minutes, when we got there, clapping his hands in ecstatic appreciation of the old M.G. It occurred to me that he might be spinning things out mainly to re-arrange the number he had first thought of, having now woken up to the fact that, since he was carrying neither brief case nor parcel, it would be a tricky business explaining to Andy that he had spent the whole afternoon gathering up sheaves of vital documents.

Lorraine was in the kitchen, which looked as though Typhoon Milly had just passed through on a dry run. She was throwing together a dinner of clam soup, boeuf en daube, with squab farcies, for the current beloved, who was a lawyer named Henry.

'Practically everyone in Washington turns out to be a lawyer,' I remarked.

'You're so right,' she agreed, 'and practically everyone who isn't needs one.'

'Well, since you appear to need this particular one rather badly, it may come as a relief to hear that I'll be out for dinner this evening.'

'Want me to fetch you?' she asked. 'Or will they bring you home after?'

'Since it's Toby, I'd say that was most unlikely, but he's at the Watergate, so I anticipate no difficulty in picking up a cab.'

'Oh, in that case . . . but from now on the problem needn't bother us because I've had a great idea. Listen, Tessa, do you have a licence to drive in this country? You do? Well, that's very good news because I've arranged it so you're going to be using the M.G. and no harm in starting off within the law.'

'But, Lorraine, I couldn't do that. I'd be scared stiff.'

'No, you wouldn't, it's not half so terrifying as driving in London or Paris.'

'What about the dreaded pollution?'

'We'll have to put that in cold storage for a while. It's a question of first priorities. If you have the car I'll be able to sleep nights when you're out, and also get on with my practising without having to look at my watch every five minutes, wondering whether you're stranded somewhere with a gun in your back. Besides, you'll look terrific in it! Tomorrow I'll buy you an Afghan hound to go in the passenger seat. Only thing is, though, you can't take it tonight. There's a trick about the brakes which no one but me understands and even I am liable to forget. Also the battery's down. Tomorrow I'll get it all fixed up like new and away you'll go!'

Lorraine, for whom every new scheme had to run its course, was soon carried away by this one, but abruptly switched off when she noticed the time and realised that Henry, the most punctual of lawyers, was due in half an hour. In the two minutes' limbo, before the boeuf en daube took full possession again, I managed to broach the subject of a migraine specialist and she promised to come up with an answer the next day. Having placed a foot in this door, I went to my bedroom, the larger of the two upstairs rooms and overlooking the tiny garden, blissfully unaware that one further step had been taken in paving the way for the catastrophes ahead.

CHAPTER EIGHT

1

IF TUESDAY'S rehearsal had been stormy, it was a gavotte compared to the one on the following afternoon. Up to the lunch break things had gone tolerably well, but once again, when Gilbert joined us for the afternoon session, he was a character much changed for the worse. It was particularly unfortunate that he should have arrived punctually, for once, because he was just in time to hear the end of one of Hugo's more brilliant tours de force. This was an imaginary, but all too credible monologue in which Gilbert explained to Andy that the play would have so much more impact if the entire cast, with the exception of himself, were to perform in masks.

The ill temper which resulted soon reached such a pitch that I was inclined to wonder whether Andy had not indeed underestimated the nervous strain that Gilbert was suffering and whether, when it came to the crunch, he would be fit to go on at all.

However, as I was soon to discover, the evil mood did not derive solely from nerves. Terry was my informant. Apart from a brief excursion in search of slightly more edible luncheon snacks than he had previously laid on, he had spent the day glued, in a martyred fashion, to the type-writer and this diligence had paid off because he was alone in the office when the telegram arrived from London and alone there, with Gilbert, when it was opened. The signatory was Daphne and she stated briefly, but with no possibility of a misunderstanding, that she would be landing at Dulles Airport at eight-thirty, our time, that evening.

Toby was highly amused when I broke the news to him at our rendezvous in the shady bar. It transpired that after leaving me the previous night he had met Gilbert, returning from the evening's revelries and had joined him in a night-cap. Gilbert had been in a mellow mood and, having assured Toby that he was the one truly intelligent and civilised man of his acquaintance, had proceeded to put these qualities to the test by confessing that he had found true love at last and was about to plight his troth with a lady from Connecti-cut. Furthermore, she was all set to plight hers back, just as soon as their respective divorce proceedings were put in hand, for it turned out that this female was not the sister of the young man who was being brought in to assist Terry, but his mother and the partner in the marriage, so Toby informed me, with most of the millions.

'I don't know what's so funny,' I told him, when he had finished falling about. 'You wouldn't be laughing if you'd been with us this afternoon and I should have thought you had as much to lose as anyone if we flop.'

'Oh, don't talk so daft, Tessa, you don't have to worry about Gilbert. All this huffing and puffing must be very trying for you, I admit, but it's only his way of keeping himself in trim. He's a professional, first and last, and he'll be a knock out, just you wait and see! On and off stage too; you'll all be drinking champagne out of his shoes after the opening night. I've seen it happen so often.'

'Including Daphne?'

'Yes, Daphne too, if that's the way he decides to play it, although it will be interesting to watch him going to work there. She's a tough egg, old Daph. I suppose she's heard the news about Gilbert's romance and is bringing her hatchet over to break it up. What time does she get in?'

'In about three hours from now,' I said, peering at my watch in the flame of my cigarette lighter.

'And Gilbert is meeting her?'

'In person. The original plan was to send Terry along, but someone talked him out of that. Or perhaps he realised it would be the sort of snub to make her even more belligerent. Another idea is that he may have hopes of persuading her to take the next plane home again.'

'Not a chance,' Toby said, 'and I can hardly wait for the next instalment. Shall we do some morse code with our torches and get the waitress to bring us another of these?'

'No thanks, I have to get back and see what Lorraine has been able to fix about a doctor. It seems Rose is no better and I think Catherine is in quite a stew, underneath the grande dame manner. I've promised to let her know something this evening. One way and another, the domestic lives of our two stars tend to govern all our movements at present.'

2

There was a gap in the line of cars outside Number 1312A, signifying two facts; the first that Lorraine had carried out her threat of taking the M.G. to be overhauled, and the second that this had happened too recently for any prowling Georgetown driver to have seized upon the empty space.

Nothing wrong, so far, and the first intimations of trouble came when I tilted the flower pot and my fingers, groping for the key, brushed over bare and dusty stone. I hauled the urn sideways, so that the whole dark ring where it had rested was revealed and that too was bare. I stood upright again, one part of my mind debating whether to try some of the other pots, the other already resigned to the horrid truth, that love had conquered all recollection of my existence and Lorraine had gone prancing off with Henry and the key, leaving me locked out for the evening. Curiously enough, the more obvious explanation did not occur to me until, gazing in mute despair at the front door, as though imploring it to give me a message, it obligingly did so, informing me that it was not completely closed.

Even then, the immediate sensation was one of relief, for I concluded that Lorraine was indoors, perhaps at work on an étude and therefore unable to hear the bell. Why she should first have removed the key was a question I instantly dismissed, for it was useless to expect rational behaviour from Lorraine, who invariably had highly logical reasons to account for her highly eccentric behaviour and it was not until I attempted to push the door wider open and found that it would only move about a foot, before jamming up against some heavy object, that what might be described as naked fear, or at any rate naked bewilderment set in.

I pushed with all my strength, knowing how futile it was, then pressed my face into the narrow opening and peered inside. The hall lamp had not been switched on and the only natural light came from the glass door on to the garden, in the sitting room. It was too faint to illuminate the scene in the hall in any detail, but I could just discern that the object barring my way was an upended bicycle wheel and that beyond it there was a dark and shapeless mound, alarmingly similar in shape to a supine human form.

I withdrew my head and, with a calm which I now find slightly unnatural, pondered the next move. There was no simple solution because I had no idea where to look for a telephone booth and one of the most notable features of American cities, particularly when night falls, is the dearth of pedestrians. Looking in both directions, I could see no one on the street at all, so I went next door and banged as loudly as I could, at the same time keeping a finger pressed on the bell. It was a fatuous way to behave because another feature of American city life is the marked reluctance of the inhabitants to respond to loud bangs and pealing bells. However, there were only the regulation three or four lights on, and seemingly no television going, so the owners were probably not at home in any case.

Bogged down in this impasse and painfully aware that every second wasted could make the difference between life and death for Lorraine, my mind kept returning to the scene it had constructed of her lying face down in the hall, with a bullet wound in her head and the blood flowing unchecked and, picturing it yet again, I mentally raised my eyes and saw, above and beyond her dark shape, the pale shaft of light from the garden window. I knew it to be fitted up with all the usual safety gadgets, but Lorraine rarely bothered to put them into operation during the daytime, so there was a good chance that it was still unlocked and, more important still, that the wire screen had not been drawn across.

It did not take long to verify this because at the bottom of Lorraine's garden there was a grassy mound, once the site of a graveyard and now an occasional haunt for smashed out drunks and junkies and, on its highest point, a small Episcopal church, whose entrance was on the parallel street, two blocks from where I was standing. Lorraine had described the terrain to me, pointing it out as a short cut to the Public Library and also a French delicatessen, both of which figured largely in her life. I felt confident that by taking the long way round I should have no difficulty in finding the short cut back through the garden.

As it happened, I did pass one or two people, as I pelted down the first street and then half-way along the right angled one, but they all looked as though they didn't want to know and I was not tempted to enlist their help, believing that it would achieve nothing, apart from frightening them to death.

It was the right decision too because I could tell, as I ran down the tangled grassy slope towards the hedge, that the screen door was not in place and that I should be able to get in by breaking the glass, if necessary. It was not, however, for the inner door slid open at a touch and, throwing my bag on to a chair, so as to leave both hands free, I began feeling my way round for a light switch.

Lorraine was indeed lying face down, her attitude very much as I had imagined it, but there was no bullet and very little blood. Nor was her skull crushed in. On the contrary, it had expanded a bit, for there was a lump the size of a golf ball just below the crown. Her breathing, though noisy, was regular and the indications were that she had sustained nothing worse than concussion. All the same, I knew better than to try and move her, although I did manage to extricate the bicycle, part of which had become tangled up in her legs, with the back half sticking up in the air, like some grotesque version of the spinning wheel in the fairy tale.

Having achieved this much, I was somewhat at a loss as to disposing of the bike, for the porch was too narrow to hold it and the hallway already overcrowded to suffocation point. In the end I opened the front door, rested the handle-bar against it and left the rear end sticking out over the sill. Then I went upstairs to fetch a blanket for Lorraine and, finally, applying myself to the telephone, was immediately confronted by fresh problems.

It had been my intention to dial 911, which I had been told was the number to contact in such emergencies, but the enforced delay, combined with the fact that Lorraine's injuries did not appear to be so very dreadful, had induced second thoughts. In the first place, I had no idea what happened to people who were hauled away by the public services, whether they were well cared for and given the right treatment, and secondly I quailed at the prospect of the bleating and yowling of the ambulance and police cars, as they hurtled up the narrow street, having heard them going about their business numerous times already and finding the sound both grisly and alarming. Seeking for some other alternative, I thumbed my way through the scrawled pages of Lorraine's telephone pad, hoping to find the number of her private doctor there, or even a more recent entry referring to a migraine specialist, which would have been better than nothing.

It was during this search that I heard footsteps on the porch and was cursing myself for not having ditched the bike and locked the front door when I heard a voice exclaiming in cultivated tones: 'JEEsus Christ!', and went into the hall to find a strange man standing there, with such an expression of horror and astonishment on his face as to declare him instantly to be none other than Henry.

He was very handsome and clean cut and, in addition to this, proved Lorraine's point up to the hilt about the advantages of knowing a good lawyer, because from the moment of his taking charge it all became plain sailing. For a start, he was a patient listener and heard my confused and incoherent tale to the end, without interruption, at the same time feeling Lorraine's pulse and smoothing back her hair in the most calm and competent fashion, in itself reassuring, and he nodded agreement to my suggestion that she was not badly injured.

'I'd say you were right, Tessa. God Almighty, you have to be right! Listen, why don't you fetch a pillow for her head, while I call my doctor? He prefers to see the patients in his office, but I think I have ways to make him relax the rule, for once.'

I hastened to obey, having no doubt at all that he was right.

3

Lorraine opened her eyes briefly during the first stage of our vigil, even mumbling a few words between groans, to the effect that she felt fine, fine, never better, before passing out again. Encouraged by this, we hauled her on to the sofa, so that she could be unconscious in comfort.

The doctor exceeded expectations by arriving within fifteen minutes and soon afterwards Henry and I moved on to our next port in the storm, which was a bar round the corner from the hospital where Lorraine had been taken for patching up and X-rays.

In this more relaxed atmosphere and cheered by the preliminary report on the patient's condition, we began to speculate about what had happened.

'It's fairly obvious, isn't it,' I said, 'that whoever attacked her was already in the house? Presumably, he heard her open the front door and crept out to knock her unconscious before she could raise the alarm. Which reminds me: we ought to get the lock changed right away, because he still has the key.'

'No, he doesn't,' Henry said, bringing it out of his pocket. 'I found it in the gutter where I parked my car. He must have thrown it down just before he ran off.'

'Well, that was considerate, anyway.'

'Or prudent, maybe. If he were picked up later, on some other deal, it wouldn't help him too much to be found with another person's latch key on him. What worries me, Tessa, is how he would have known how to find it, in the first place?'

'But that's easy, isn't it? I know Lorraine insists that it's more convenient to keep it under the urn than to risk being locked out when she forgets to take one with her, but the system certainly simplified matters for any thief who happened to be keeping the house under observation.'

Henry frowned at me in rather a severe way: 'So you consider this was a planned job, that this guy had been watching the house, had familiarised himself with Muriel's work schedule and had only to wait for Lorraine to be out to make the break in?'

'Exactly!' I said, thinking that proceedings in American courts must be fairly spun out if all lawyers spent so much time recounting the obvious.

'Burglarisation being the objective?'

'Precisely.'

'Then how come he was still there when Lorraine got back?'

'I beg your pardon? I don't follow you.'

'Don't apologise,' Henry said kindly. 'Not being a professional criminal yourself, or even a native of this land, you couldn't be expected to know, but here's how it normally goes: anyone who has taken that amount of pains to familiarise himself with the territory and to have chosen his moment, would not be likely to waste time in hanging around. He would have been in there like a streak, snatching up what he came for and, in all probability, out on the street again inside three minutes. They work fast, these boys, you have to believe me, and that is the maximum period of time he would have needed.'

'Yes, but supposing she'd returned in less than three minutes? You know, forgotten something and had to come back for it?'

'In my assessment, if he had had the house under surveillance over a period of time, it is certainly a contingency he would have allowed for. When did you ever know her go out without leaving something behind? But you also have to remember that she was using the bike and not her car. Whichever direction she would have taken, it would be five minutes before she would be out of sight and this would give him a minimum of five minutes in which to operate before she could return. However, I regard this as speculation on the academic level, since we can fairly make the assumption that it is based on a false premise.'

'Oh, can we? Why is that?'

'Well, you see, Tessa, if she had returned for the purpose of collecting something she had forgotten, she wouldn't have planned on spending more than a couple of minutes fetching it; just long enough to pick up her purse or whatever; isn't that right?'

'And?'

'And so, in those circumstances, she would almost without doubt have left the bicycle down on the sidewalk. Conceivably, she would have pulled it half-way up the steps. What she would not have done, in her wildest aberration, was to have dragged it the whole way into the house. Furthermore, the noise would have been sufficient to alert a deaf man who was fast asleep and our guy would have been out of there, through the glass door into the yard, before she even knew he existed.'

'Then why didn't he?'

'Pardon me?'

'Why didn't he escape through the garden window? It wasn't locked and he didn't even have to stop and pull back the screen. Whether he was taken off guard or not, why pile on trouble for himself by going into the hall at all?'

'I would conclude it was because he was already there.'

'On the point of leaving, you mean?'

'No, on the point of arriving. In my view, the most probable train of events was that he followed her to the house and got his foot jammed inside the door while she was stacking up the bike, intending to scare her into handing over her money and whatever jewellery she happened to be wearing. But Lorraine doesn't scare that easy and she can be pretty quick off the mark, as you are aware. She may have struck him first or acted in some way so that he was the one to lose his nerve and he knocked her cold, primarily to give himself time to get away.'

'So not a professional, pre-meditated job, after all?'

'Not for my money. He can't have been armed, otherwise she would have known better than to stand up to him and we wouldn't have found that diamond ring on her finger, or the bills still in her purse.'

'So you believe it was some lunatic acting on impulse?'

'Right. An impulse arising out of previous experience, maybe, but not set up in advance. And I don't throw this out only for the reasons I've enumerated, Tessa. There's another circumstance which in my opinion proves it conclusively.'

'What's that?'

'Nothing had been touched. I had a careful look around while we were waiting for Dr Matheson and her radio and television and things of that kind were all where they should have been. If he'd been alone in the house for even two minutes, I question whether he would have spent the time just admiring them.'

I considered my reply carefully, debating whether to tell him of a small discovery of my own which had some bearing on this, but decided that it was not the moment. This was partly because the theory he had worked out was so neat and comforting that I was reluctant to spoil it and partly from a desire to spare him anxiety about Lorraine's future safety. So instead of answering directly, I said:

'Will you tell the police?'

He shook his head: 'What can they do? Lorraine may be able to tell us whether this joker was young or old, black or white, but I doubt she'll be able to recall any more than that. It's not too much to go on and furthermore there's not such a hell of a lot to charge him with. Hopefully, her injuries are not serious and there's no involvement of larceny. We really don't have much of a case.'

I was more than ever tempted to tell him what I had found when I went into Lorraine's bedroom to fetch the blanket, but he was already signalling for the bill and as soon as it was brought to him he threw down some notes and stood up.

'Come on, baby! Time to get back to the hospital and find out what's going on. Then I'll drive you home.'

'Thanks,' I said bleakly, this being one prospect I had deliberately closed my mind to all through dinner.

'Cheer up!' he said, gauging my feelings correctly. 'I'll come all the way inside with you and we'll check through every last nook and cranny. And there's one thing we most certainly will not do.'

'What's that?'

'Put the key back under that darned urn. Lorraine can squawk all she likes, but from now on that's out.'

CHAPTER NINE

1

'HE CERTAINLY is the most awfully dear man and I quite understand why Lorraine dotes on him,' I told Toby, when reporting on these events by telephone the next morning. 'Having turned the place inside out, he saw that I was still bothered about having to spend the night here on my own, so he insisted on making up a bed for himself on the sofa. It was very noble of him because he's a tall man and he must have been most uncomfortable.'

'And a fairly silly man too, if I may say so. Why didn't he use Lorraine's room?'

'Perhaps he thought it would be rather insensitive to do that while she lies wounded in hospital. Also he may have thought it would compromise me, in some way, if we were both asleep on the same landing. He is very much of the old school.'

'Oh yes, and I think American men must rather enjoy sleeping on sofas,' Toby said. 'I seem to remember sitting through reels and reels where they did practically nothing else.'

'You may be a little out of date there,' I suggested.

'You could be right. It is some years now since I ventured inside a cinema. Still, it's comforting to find that the convention lives on, in real life if nowhere else. Is this Rock Hudson still with you?'

'No. I went down to get some coffee just now and found a note on the piano, giving his home and office numbers and instructions to call him if I felt the teensiest bit nervous, in which case he'd be back on the sofa again tonight. You must admit they can be fantastically kind.'

'And fantastically officious too. Since when have you needed all this protection? Flirting with danger used to be all the go with you. Besides, I see no reason why this person should bother you again. He is probably just someone with a fetish about women on bicycles.'

'Yes, that's more or less Henry's attitude, but I have a nasty feeling there's more to it than that. I happen to know something which he doesn't.'

'That would never surprise me.'

'I'm convinced the man was already in the house when Lorraine got there. You see, Toby, when I went to get a blanket from her bed I got a fearful jolt because her room was really chaotic. I know she's chronically untidy and disorganised, but it's hard to believe that she would have left it in that state. Also yesterday was a Muriel morning and she would certainly have tidied it before she left. She's the kind who follows you from room to room with a duster in her hand, snatching up the ashtray before you've finished stubbing out the cigarette.'

'All the same, Lorraine was more than capable of undoing all her work at a later stage. For instance, if she was late for an appointment and had to change in a hurry . . .'

'She didn't change; in a hurry or otherwise. When I found her unconscious in the hall she was still wearing the same pair of jeans she'd had on in the morning. And there's another thing, Toby.'

'It sounds as though you were on form, after all. Being abroad hasn't dulled your passion for seeking out the sinister.'

'Don't you want to hear about it?'

'I can hardly wait,' he replied, smothering a yawn.

'There was a sort of crazy pattern in the upheaval. Naturally, I've straightened it now, because I didn't want Lorraine to come home and find it like that, but I can still picture it as it was and on the left of the room everything had been ransacked. Her closet door was open and there were things chucked about on the floor, and it was the same with the drawers in her bedside table, but nothing on the other side, including her desk incidentally, had been touched. Now, doesn't that suggest to you that he was looking for something in particular and was interrupted in midstream and doesn't it completely wash out Henry's theory that he followed her into the house?'

'No.'

'Why not?'

'He could have searched the room after he'd knocked her out and, having found what he came for when he was only half-way round, took it and went away.'

'Well, yes, I admit that's possible, but what on earth could it have been?'

'My dear Tessa, how do you expect me to answer that? A cache of money or jewellery, or some such thing.'

'She doesn't possess any valuable jewellery, apart from that one ring she was wearing, and she's the last person in the world to keep bundles of notes stashed under the mattress.'

'Then I don't see that you have any cause for concern. Either he realised he'd picked the wrong house and gave up, or else he was the man from the C.I.A., looking for incriminating documents and, having found them, will have no reason to return. What are your plans for today?'

In my opinion, there were several flaws in his argument, including the one that no burglar worth his salt would have left by the front entrance when the back one was so much more accessible; still less, having left by the back, trouble himself to make the long journey round simply in order to replace the key outside the house. However, I could tell that, so far as Toby was concerned, the subject was now exhausted and I said:

'Spending most of it at the theatre. Only a week to go before the dress rehearsal, may I remind you? If I get away in time I'll go and see Lorraine. I rang up the hospital, by the way and she's going on a treat. Sitting up in her lace jacket and eating a boiled egg. They'll let her out tomorrow. How about you? What will you be up to?'

'If Gilbert's tied up, I might take Daphne out to lunch. You don't happen to know where she's staying?'

'Down the passage from you, presumably. I imagine he wouldn't have the nerve to put her in a separate hotel?'

'Oh yes, he would. I rang the desk just now and they've never heard of her.'

'You don't say! So perhaps after all he did persuade her to turn round and go home again?'

'That doesn't sound like my Daphne, she's made of sterner stuff. The iron hand in the iron glove. Ring me up, if you collect any gossip. I'll be here for an hour or two.'

I promised to do so, but, due to circumstances beyond my control, forgot all about it within half an hour of replacing the receiver.

2

Anxiety on Lorraine's behalf having now cooled down, the main preoccupation was how to break the news to Catherine that I had entirely failed to come up with a doctor for Rose. It is odd how often these attempts to curry favour lead to such doom laden results and the situation was rendered even more ticklish by the fact that I dared not play up the previous night's adventures as an excuse for my omission, since this would inevitably provoke smug looks from Rose and land me in a double humiliation.

It was a tricky one and no mistake, but the problem was temporarily pushed into the background when I went into Terry's office and was confronted by a vision of loveliness calling itself Harrison Engelberg Junior and allowed myself two guesses as to what he was doing there.

He was a bold and handsome young man, of about twenty-three or four, wearing royal blue and white check trousers, a pale blue cashmere pullover and clumpy white golf shoes, which added a superfluous inch or two to his height. The only slight flaw was that his head seemed disproportionately small, but this effect may have been due to his hair being smooth and shorn as a skin-diver's. Altogether an eye-on-the-ball and main-chance type, in dramatic contrast to Terry, who managed to look simultaneously flabby and tight-lipped and was seated at the typewriter with his elbows propped on the desk and his hands drooping from the wrists, in the style of a pianist loosening up for the attack on Rachmaninoff.

'Okay, I'll get busy on that right away,' Harrison said in smooth, self-confident tones, when the introductions had been completed and he had grasped my hand as though it was his favourite putter. 'Shouldn't take more than an hour and when I get back we could maybe run through the script a couple of times? Gilbert maintains I can pick it up as I go along, sitting in on rehearsals, but personally I feel I would have more to contribute, literary-wise, if I were to familiarise myself with the rhythm and tempo in advance, if you get what I mean?'

Terry neither affirmed nor denied it and Harrison saluted us both and slid off with the lithe grace of a panther.

'People here seem to have a mania for familiarising themselves with everything,' I remarked. 'It's the key word.'

'It's the key bore,' Terry replied mournfully. 'Enough to drive you starkers.'

'What's he doing here, anyway?' I asked, wondering if Terry had familiarised himself with the answer to the same extent as the rest of us. Apparently not, for he replied indifferently:

'Oh, some ploy of Gilbert's, wouldn't you know? The lad is writing his school play or something and wants to spend a few days tagging along with us and getting clued up on the technicalities. Gilbert wraps it up in a lot of treacle about him being the dog's-body and taking some of the donkey work off my shoulders; makes you feel you're working in a menagerie, doesn't it? I bet there's a dash of the old graft there somewhere, though. Has to be. Anyway, it's only for a week, thank God. Pretty he may be, but any more of that get-up-and-go lark and the only place I'd be fit for is the old donkey's rest home. You heard about Daphne?'

'Only that she's not staying at the same hotel.'

'Understatement, duckie, she's not staying in the same continent. Never showed up and Gilbert's hair turned white overnight. Behaving as though it was all my fault too, and there was I, giving up half my evening strewing red roses round his hotel suite, at his command. Wanted to take the edge off her temper, I suppose, and all wasted, you see!'

'How fascinating, Terry! Though I can't see what he's got to be annoyed about. Yesterday he was groaning because she was coming, so now he ought to be dancing for joy, surely?'

'The trouble is he's been taken for a big, bumpy old ride. He not only spent a rotten afternoon in anticipation of her arrival, he also had to drag himself out to the airport and be made to look a perfect fool when she wasn't on the plane. There were some reporters around too, so to make it look good he had to pretend to be awfully worried and disappointed and he even found it necessary to hang about for another hour or two, in case she'd switched to a different flight. He got back into town about midnight and put a call through to London to ask what she was playing at, but it was five a.m. their time and she wasn't terribly pleased.'

'What was her explanation?'

'Giving it to you in more refined language, she denied having sent any cable, said she'd never contemplated coming over and hoped he'd get off the line right this minute because she'd just got home from a party and needed her sleep. Actually, he didn't favour me with all these details. I happened to overhear him telling Andy about it.'

'What do you make of it, though? Did you actually see the cable?'

'Couldn't avoid it, dear. He was so beside himself that he flung it down like a hot cinder, practically under my nose. It came through Western Union and unless we're all going mad it stated categorically that she was on her way.'

'Where was it sent from?'

'Chelsea, which is where they live. That doesn't prove a thing, though, does it? From what I hear of Daphne and the company she keeps, it's the kind of joke that would appear too hilarious for any words after a good party, specially if she'd heard rumours that he was straying a bit. Talking of that, I have another tiny idea who might have sent it.'

So had I, as it happened, but I allowed Terry to go first.

'I've a sneaking feeling that it might have been Harrison.'

'Your donkey dog's-body? Why ever should he?'

'One or two small hints that have been thrown around in my hearing,' Terry said smugly. 'It wouldn't absolutely astonish me to find that Gilbert had got the wrong end of the stick with that one. He sees himself as the full Lord Bountiful, finding this little niche for his protégée, but I get the impression that Harrison is not overjoyed about the set up with his Mum. If you ask me, his real object in coming here was to move in close and break it up.'

'Sending that cable wouldn't have been a particularly clever move. Admittedly, it caused a certain amount of heart failure, but it's all fizzled out again, so where's the advantage?'

'It didn't fizzle out until after the reporters had got hold of it, darling, as you'll see in the afternoon paper. Mummy Engelberg will be reading it too, you may be sure, and I daresay it won't bring wedding bells any nearer when she learns how he spent all that time waiting on tenterhooks for Auntie Daph. Perhaps the young master is out to wreck things, in which case he may have a few more tricks up his sleeve,' Terry concluded in rather wistful tones.

In my personal view, he was in for a disappointment if he relied on Harrison to upset Gilbert's apple cart, but, strangely enough, only a few hours later it began to look as though he might have grounds for believing it, after all. This was when my own candidate for practical joker became the apparent victim of one himself and Hugo failed to turn up for rehearsal.

Things went on tolerably well without him at first because we were doing scene two of the second act, in which he only appeared briefly, but later we moved on to scene three, where he and Gilbert had a long dialogue and things deteriorated rapidly. On Gilbert's insistence, Harrison was brought in to read Hugo's part, which he did excessively badly, throwing himself into it with everything he had and giving the ham performance of the century, thereby effectively ruining Gilbert's timing and making a shambles of the entire scene.

This was naturally very trying for Gilbert and not made any less so by the fact that Catherine evidently found it rather amusing. Afterwards, Gilbert vented his fury on Andy, who promptly unloaded it on to Terry, commanding him to find Hugo within the next ten minutes, even if it meant dragging the Potomac personally and by hand.

Terry made a valiant attempt to revenge himself on the receptionist at Hugo's hotel, but, lacking the expertise of the other two, got his come-uppance three times over, in dulcet but implacable tones. The gist, as relayed to Andy, was as follows:

Hugo had left his hotel, alone and on foot, at approximately nine-thirty, a telephone call from the theatre having been connected to his room some minutes earlier. On departing, he had mentioned that he would not be back until the afternoon, as his rehearsal had been cancelled and he proposed to board a tourist coach and spend the morning at Mount Vernon. On hearing this, Andy advised Terry to go to Mount Vernon himself, among other less salubrious places that occurred to him, and returned to take it out on all the rest of us by putting us through our paces in act two, scene two, all over again.

Rehearsals limped along through the remainder of the morning session, with nerves and tempers growing increasingly frayed and the first to snap was Jackie. Overcome by the tension which now afflicted the whole company in greater or lesser degree, she first missed her entrance, then fluffed her lines and finally dried up completely in the face of Gilbert's lip curling scorn, before bursting into noisy, hysterical tears.

Since Gilbert's contempt had been expressed in looks and not words and since in any case his annoyance was amply justified, there was nothing that Clive could do in his wife's defence, beyond turning ashen pale and muttering ferociously under his breath, all of which was closely observed by a smiling Harrison, who was now watching the proceedings from the fifth row of the stalls. So far as I could tell, he did not miss a trick and I began to reconsider Terry's imputation that his had been the hand behind the bogus telegram. Moreover, it was entirely credible that he was responsible for the false message to Hugo, for if Terry had made such a mistake he would surely have taken immediate steps to rectify it. Although incurably inefficient and disorganised, he was not completely off his head and, rightly or wrongly, believed he had as much to lose as any of us by the play's failure.

At two o'clock we broke at last and Andy advised us all to take a rest before returning at seven for the lighting rehearsal. At this point I finally nerved myself to approach Catherine, who was packing up her basket in preparation for departure, and to mumble my apologies for having failed to find a specialist for Rose. However, like many hurdles which loom so formidably in the imagination, this one turned out to be two inches high and to be made of sponge. Evidently, she had never taken my offer seriously, nor placed any reliance on it whatever. She graciously informed me that there was nothing for me to worry about because Rose was recovering. She had elected to spend the morning resting at home because they were planning a shopping expedition in the afternoon, to choose a present for Rose's mother, who was about to celebrate her eightieth birthday.

'This afternoon? Won't you be awfully tired, Miss Fuller?'

'Ty . . . ahd?' she repeated, savouring the word as though she could hardly wait to look it up in the dictionary. 'No, but you're looking peaky, you know, dear. You mustn't allow yourself to be ruffled by these little contretemps. Sail through, that's my motto in life. Keep your nose to the grindstone and sail through! Doesn't that conjure up a charming picture? And I daresay you'll manage it too. I always say that you have more stamina than most of your generation. Poor little Jackie now, a dear, sweet child and brimming over with talent, I feel sure, but she'll never do if she makes a habit of going to pieces when things are not quite as she would wish. One needs the hide of a rhinoceros in this game. Well, my dear, I do hope your poor friend will soon be better. Some bullying person knocked her down outside her own front door, they tell me. Do tell her how sorry I am.'

'Oh, thank you, I will. I'm going to see her this afternoon and she'll be awfully thrilled to have a message from you.'

Catherine smiled benignly down at me: 'And let it be a lesson to you, my child. One cannot be too careful these days. Simply no knowing what people will get up to next!'

How true!

3

It would have been a comparatively encouraging note to end the day on, but unfortunately a number of calamities still remained on the list it had drawn up for us and the five minutes spent talking to Catherine delayed me just long enough to ensure my participation in the next one.

The first intimations of something amiss came when I stepped out of the lift, on my way to collect some oddments from my dressing room, and met Gilbert coming out of Jackie's room, which was next to mine. He was looking very amused and relaxed and, although there was a hint in the way he kept one hand firmly holding back the lift door, that he was in sufficient hurry not to let it rise again without him, he nonetheless detained me in a bit of friendly chat and commiseration.

'Horrid for you, my darling! All this violence is quite a worry, isn't it? And so disappointing to find that one does have to believe everything one reads in the papers. How did it happen? No, better not tell me; you must be bored stiff with describing it all and one doesn't want to be morbid.'

To my gratified amazement, he then went on to speak quite seriously about Lorraine, saying how much he had admired her and also sounding genuinely concerned about my own safety, expressing himself with such artistry that it was impossible to doubt his sincerity, and capping it all by asking very kindly after Robin, whose existence was seldom acknowledged by my other colleagues, since, having no connection with the play, it was rarely even remembered.

I was much moved and in those few minutes he endeared himself to me as effectively as most people could have contrived to do in as many weeks. Temporarily, at any rate, he was my truest, most understanding friend in all the world and the first one I would turn to if I were ever in a jam.

Doubtless, it would not have taken long to come down from the clouds and see the incident for precisely what it was, but this cooling down process got off to a head start and the soppy smile was wiped clean off my face when I approached my dressing room and heard one hell of a rumpus going on next door. Plainly, Jackie and Clive were in the throes of an earth shattering row, for he was shouting at the top of his lungs and she was responding with high pitched, wailing sobs. It was rather unnerving, but obviously no business of mine and I should have snatched up the belongings I had come for and made a bolt for it, had not Clive come flying out of his wife's room, white with passion and practically knocking me flat in his rush towards the lifts. He had been in too much of a hurry or too incensed to close the door behind him and I could see Jackie slumped over the jars and pots on her dressing table, her shoulders heaving like an ocean swell and her distress now taking the form of loud and agonised groans. I wanted to shut the door and leave her to recover in private, but she must have heard me, for she jerked her head up and stared momentarily at my reflection in her mirror. She did not speak and her head drooped again, but at the same time she flapped one hand in a beckoning gesture and I went inside and closed the door.

The groaning continued at full spate for several minutes, but I suspected that she was consciously timing it and, considering it wiser not to cut her short, restrained myself with as much forbearance as I could, trying not to count the hours left to me for fitting in a visit to Lorraine, let alone for getting a rest before the lighting rehearsal. Other thoughts which obtruded, as patience wore thinner, were that it was certainly going to provide a challenge for Marty if she went on blotching up her face at this rate and also that it was a pity that some of the emotional energy could not be channelled into her work, instead of boring the pants off other people. However, she brought these uncharitable reflections to an end at last by subsiding into snorts and sniffles, pawing blindly at the box of tissues.

'Better now?' I asked, pushing a pile of them into her hand.

'Yes . . . I think so. Sorry to be such a . . . bore, Tessa.'

'That's all right. Anything I can do?'

'Nothing anyone can do,' she replied with another shuddering sob; then added in tones of quiet desperation: 'It's all right, I shan't break down again. And thanks.'

'What for?'

'Oh, just for being here. For standing by. God knows what I might have done if I'd been left on my own, but I'll be able to pull out of it now.'

'Oh, good!'

'It's no use giving way, I see that. I've simply got to face up to it and come to terms.'

'Quite right! So you'll be okay now?' I suggested, edging towards the door, although knowing in my heart that it would not be so easy as that.

'Don't you think,' she asked me in a sharper voice, 'that of all the deadly sins jealousy is the most despicable and destructive?'

'Oh, every time.'

'Specially when it's so totally unfounded. I mean, God knows, it's practically unbelievable.'

'What is?'

'Clive's behaviour. You couldn't begin to imagine the things he said. I was deeply shocked, if you want to know. I had no idea he had this dark side to his nature.'

'Cheer up! I expect he's got over it by now, whatever was bothering him and he'll be back in a minute to kiss and make up.'

'Never!' she replied in haughty, Mrs Siddons tones and with eyes which no doubt flashed a thousand sparks, if one could have seen them behind the puffed up lids. 'Never, never, never! There are some things one can't forgive and lack of trust is one of them. I shall never speak to him again.'

Realising now that this True Confession would take all night if I allowed her to practise every trick in her repertoire, I said resignedly:

'At a guess, all this has something to do with Gilbert, but I feel I should warn you, Jackie . . .'

She interrupted me, betraying the first hint of spontaneity:

'Why do you presume that?'

'Because I met him coming out of here just now. He looked mighty pleased with himself, which usually means bad news for someone, but you must remember that we're all a bit strung up just now and liable to break out for no particular reason. If Gilbert's been teasing you, or trying to mix it, you must keep your cool and not take it out on Clive, for goodness' sake. That can't help anything.'

'You couldn't be more mistaken,' she replied, picking up a hairbrush and shaking out her dark mane before going to work on it. 'It's quite ludicrous how wrong you are! Gilbert hasn't been mixing it at all, he couldn't have been more angelic. He actually took the trouble to come and apologise for being such a brute to me this morning. How about that? And he was fantastically kind and understanding. He spent ages explaining to me that he doesn't really mean to be beastly, but he can only work at full pressure when everyone's keyed up to fever pitch. And he also said that sometimes the only way to get the best out of people, so they can realise their own potential, is to reduce them to the lowest possible jelly.'

'Thanks a lot.'

'It probably makes sense, Tessa. As he pointed out, he was on the stage before I was even born; only he'd realised afterwards that some people are extra sensitive and that he'd pushed me beyond the limits. That was why he came to apologise and ask me to forgive him. Which I do. Absolutely. I'll never mind in future how much he loses his temper because I've learnt how underneath all the facade he's really a very vulnerable and frightened person.'

'That could well be,' I agreed. 'Name one who isn't. But it doesn't excuse his also being spiteful, selfish and destructive and you ought to open your baby blue eyes a bit wider and ask yourself what particular game he's playing now.'

'I would expect you to adopt that attitude,' she told me, smiling smugly as she worked away at her hair in sweeping, languorous movements, 'but you don't know the first thing about it. He's actually a very sweet, dear person. Lonely, too. Did you know he had a daughter by his first wife, who's about my age, that he simply adored? He never sees her though, because his wife was so vindictive that she kept them apart and literally poisoned this girl's mind against him. Don't you find that absolutely disgusting?'

'Yes, I do, and absolutely stale and hackneyed too. Dozens of elderly actors have tried to tell me that I reminded them of their long lost daughters, or of the daughters they longed for but never had, as the case may be. It's about the oldest ploy in the game, but I gather you fell for it and tumbled straight into his fatherly embrace?'

'What a coarse thing to say, Tessa! You make it sound absolutely sordid and revolting and it wasn't like that at all. Honestly, I don't know why I bother! I could never make you understand that it wasn't just an ordinary sex thing, but something much deeper and more tender.'

'And I presume you were just plumbing these tender depths when Clive came prancing in and no doubt also found some difficulty in grasping that it wasn't just an ordinary sex thing?'

'Even so, he had no right to say what he did. You can't imagine how he went on. Like some monstrous Victorian tyrant. I was quite expecting him to invite Gilbert to step outside. It would have been funny if it hadn't been so disgusting and humiliating, but I must say Gilbert behaved beautifully. He didn't lose his temper, or shout back; he just smiled.'

'He had plenty to smile about.'

'Well, it was a damn sight more dignified than Clive's ranting and screaming. Anyway, I shall stay here until it's time for rehearsal and tonight I'll probably move into another hotel.'

'Oh, you and Clive will have made it up by then. At least, I trust you will.'

'Then you'll be disappointed. You might be able to forgive that kind of behaviour, but I happen to have rather high standards and I wouldn't contemplate spending my life with someone who's proved himself to be so despicable.'

'So which hotel were you thinking of, Jackie?'

'Oh hell, what does that matter? Honestly, you have the most prosaic mind of anyone I know. I'm sure if they told us that Armageddon was coming you'd start cutting sandwiches for it.'

'I was only thinking that by the time we get through here tonight it may be rather late to start tramping round Washington looking for an hotel room.'

'Oh well, in that case, I can go across to the Watergate. I gather one can always get a room there at short notice.'

'Oh really? And who did you gather that from?'

'Honestly, darling, your mind!'

Jackie uttered this comment without rancour and, indeed, had travelled in the space of ten minutes from a state of hopeless desolation to an almost dreamy complacency, touching down briefly at various emotional stops on the way and, in the belief that she was now coasting along so smoothly that she could safely be left to continue the journey alone, I wished her luck and went on my way.

CHAPTER TEN

LORRAINE was almost as vague about the identity of her assailant as Henry had predicted. Her only recollection of any significance was that he had been black, but since she bound me to secrecy on this, throwing out a lot of important sounding phrases like 'sensitivity areas' and 'minority groups', the information was not much use as evidence. So emphatic, indeed, was she on the need for discretion that she declared an embargo on the whole subject, that it might die down as quickly as possible and be forgotten. Curiously enough, I foresaw no difficulty in complying with this ruling because, although everyone I had spoken to on the subject had shown a proper concern and sympathy, there had been a marked reluctance to hear the details.

Strictly for my private information, she admitted retaining a strong impression of a black fuzzy head suddenly materialising between her and the sitting room, as she turned round after closing the front door and a split second before she was knocked unconscious.

This did not coincide in any way with the theory that he had followed her into the house and the mystery remained as to why he had chosen that escape route when the alternative one had been so much safer and more accessible, although one explanation for this was now beginning to take shape. Unfortunately I did not get a chance to test it out on her because the atmosphere was very snug in her little white hospital cell and I dropped off to sleep in the armchair while she was talking.

I was awakened at six by a nurse arriving with the patient's supper tray and immediately flew into a quarrelsome panic about being late for rehearsal, only calmed out of it by Lorraine's categorical assertion that if I did not instantly find a taxi she would personally telephone a friend in the White House and procure the necessary authority to have me transported to the theatre by ambulance.

Luckily, there was no need for these drastic measures, for to have arrived there to the accompaniment of those screaming sirens must surely have materially increased the spirit of alarm and apprehension with which I found the atmosphere to be already loaded. No doubt, the frustrations of the morning, combined with general fatigue, had reduced everyone to a state where even the most trifling setback was seen as a major crisis and my arrival had been preceded by two setbacks, each a little worse than trifling.

One was the unprecedented behaviour of Catherine and Rose. Normally, they came to the theatre together, whether Rose was on call or not, at least an hour in advance and went straight to Catherine's dressing room. On this occasion Catherine had arrived alone and in a most uncharacteristic fluster, having, absurdly enough, mislaid Rose. They had spent the afternoon shopping and, having completed their business, had entered a crowded lift on the fifth floor of a down town department store, which in due course fetched up at street level, where Catherine alighted and Rose did not.

Assuming that Rose had made a mistake, for she habitually forgot that in America the ground floor is called the first floor, Catherine had waited while the lift made a further descent and then came up again, and for the one next door and the one next door to that to repeat the process, but still there was no Rose among the emerging crowds. Nor was she at the apartment when Catherine eventually returned there. We learnt afterwards that the very tame explanation was that she had been overcome by heat and fatigue and had had to rush to the Ladies, but when I reached the theatre myself her whereabouts were still unknown.

All this was upsetting enough, but still more serious was the continuing absence of Hugo. Terry had been endeavouring to track him down since four o'clock, but each time he rang the hotel it was to be met with the same negative response. Either Hugo had not returned, or else he had come in and gone out again without picking up any messages. To put the lid on it, Gilbert, hearing of this and of the inevitable postponement which must result, had left the theatre in a huff, leaving word that he would return when reliably informed that he was needed.

Most of the foregoing was fed to me by Jackie, for neither Terry nor Harrison were at their posts. No one knew what Harrison was up to, but Terry had been despatched to Hugo's hotel just in case, despite their denials, he was asleep in his room.

'What do you make of it?' I asked her. 'I know Hugo's a dreadful ass in many ways, but I'd have thought this kind of behaviour was unlike him. Of course you know him much better than I do.'

'One of his silly jokes, I suppose,' Jackie replied indifferently, applying her make up in a serious and business-like
way. She alone, appeared comparatively unmoved in
this crisis, with no spark left now of the fires which had
consumed her two hours earlier and I guessed that her
passion for Gilbert was already on the wane. No doubt,
she was slightly offended by his flouncing out on his own,
without a thought for his little surrogate daughter, and it
struck me that if Clive could be prevailed upon to strew a
few roses in her path while the rebound was in full swing,
one of our minor troubles at least would be over.

Accordingly, when I left her I turned down the right
angled corridor and tapped on his door. There was no answer
and I looked inside and found the room was empty. He was
not in the Green Room either and Harrison, who had now
returned and was deep in the *Washington Star News*, told
me that he had gone for a walk.

'A walk!' he repeated in wondering tones. 'He has to be
out of his mind! It's pitch dark out there, for a start!'

Even as he spoke we heard from far away the faint wails
of the emergency services out on their gruesome business
and the usual frisson of alarm which I always experienced at
the sound took on an extra sinister dimension. The Kennedy
Center complex stands on its own small eminence, isolated
and insulated from most of the city noises and we were not
often assailed by this particular one in our ivory tower. This,
I think, can have been the only reason for our momentarily
linking it now with the fact that Clive had gone for a stroll.

Not that the connection existed, however, for he returned
within ten minutes, safe and sound, though with a strange
tale to relate. His desire for fresh air and exercise had
instinctively set him off in the direction of the river, but
he had soon realised that this would be asking for trouble
at that hour, since there was a wide, unlighted open space

between the Center and the embankment and so he had doubled back, by way of Virginia Avenue, up to 23rd Street at its intersection with New Hampshire. It was at this point that his story became curious, for he maintained, against all probability, that he had caught sight of Gilbert walking ahead of him towards Washington Circle. The street was moderately well lighted and he had recognised him both by his distinctive gait and the equally distinctive angle and shape of his hat. He had not paused to question why Gilbert should be travelling on foot, instead of in his swanky limousine, because there was a personal matter which he was anxious to discuss with him, at some place outside the theatre, and now that the chance appeared to be coming his way his mind was intent on what he was going to say.

His intention had been to catch up with Gilbert and have it out with him on the spot, but a little further on Gilbert had overturned this plan by making a sudden wheel to the left, down a narrow residential street and he had understood the reason for this when he had moved a few more paces. Straight ahead of him, some twenty yards further up the road, a solitary man was standing midway between two street lamps and well back on the sidewalk, in the shadow of a high wall. There was something strangely ominous in his stance, motionless yet alert, and in the fact that he was not looking to left or right, but straight across to the opposite side of the road. This prompted Clive to turn his head in the same direction, where, with positive alarm, he saw another man, similar in every respect, who was also apparently gazing out across the street at nothing in particular.

Following Gilbert's example, he had dived down the side street and set off at a brisk trot, although his quarry had evidently set an even faster pace, for there was still no sign of him when Clive reached the end of it, at the point where it merged through a series of islands back into Virginia

Avenue, near the north block of the Watergate. Concluding that this, after all, had been Gilbert's destination and finding, on his own admission, that the urgency of speaking to him had diminished in the light of his moment of real fear, Clive had abandoned the chase and made his way back by what he took to be the most direct route to the theatre, although in fact he had lost his bearings at one point and made a long and unnecessary detour before reaching it.

All this was related by way of apology for keeping everyone waiting, although in view of the fact that neither Hugo nor Gilbert had yet turned up, it was rather superfluous.

So this time we prepared to start the rehearsal with two members short, although as this was for lighting only and the lines immaterial, the A.S.M. would simply be required to read out the cues. It never came to that, however, for just as everything was set to begin, Harrison sauntered into the auditorium and called out to Andy that he was wanted in the office.

'For God's sake!' Andy demanded, practically whimpering with exasperation. 'Is this the moment?'

'I guess so,' Harrison replied in tones of cool, quiet authority.

'Why? Who wants me and why the hell can't Terry deal with it?'

'Terry isn't here and anyway the guy wants to see you, personally. He's called Detective Meek and he's from Homicide, so chances are he's come to report a killing.'

PART TWO

CHAPTER ONE

IT WAS Nemesis, in its crudest and most ruthless form, which, while publicly expressing it in slightly more charitable language, we all agreed. In plain words, if Hugo had not been so incurably, obsessively mean, he would have taken taxis or rented a car like everyone else, instead of beating out a well trodden path to the theatre every day and would not have ended up in a Washington gutter with a knife in his back.

It was estimated that death had been instantaneous and had occurred approximately thirty minutes before the arrival of the Deputy Medical Examiner. It was not possible to narrow it down beyond this limit because none of the residents of the lane where he was found admitted having heard or seen anything untoward. Detective Meek, when I got to know him better, told me that this was not uncommon, since most people were not about to get involved in a homicide case and could save themselves a lot of trouble by keeping their mouths shut. However, they did not all lack compassion, apparently, for on this occasion the Police Despatcher had been alerted by an anonymous telephone caller who had reported a man lying dead or injured on Prentiss Street, between 23rd and Virginia. A scout car had reached the spot within three minutes and a radio call to headquarters had brought the Deputy Medical Examiner soon afterwards. By the time the corpse had been removed to the morgue and the medical equipment been packed up, the Homicide Branch of the C.I.D. had entered the fray and taken over.

Detective Meek (this turned out to be his rank and title, as well as a job description) who had called in person to break the news that one of our cast would be permanently missing, was a square, stubby man of about forty, bullet headed and pug faced, with puzzled, sad blue eyes and, at what appeared at first sight to be an abnormal amount of russet coloured hair. Not that he wore it long; on the contrary, it was cut extremely short, but it grew lower down on his neck and in more abundance generally than on the heads of most men.

The fact that he had been able to bring the news with such speed was largely a matter of fluke, since it was believed at first that identification would be lengthy and difficult. Predictably enough, the victim's watch, cuff links and wallet had all been removed and the only remaining clue was that his jacket and shirt were of English make. However, one patrolman remembered seeing our publicity photographs in the press and it was this lever which had led to Detective Meek's calling to request Andy to accompany him to the morgue for formal identification.

'No doubt whatever,' Andy told us when he returned about an hour later, looking very green about the gills. 'Poor old Hugo! What a rotten thing to happen! I feel responsible, in an odd kind of way, although I don't know what the hell for. You can't stop a grown man from tramping around the streets at night if he has a mind to, and the ghastly, ironic thing about it is that although he always looked fairly prosperous he probably wasn't carrying more than fifty cents in that shaming little purse of his.'

'So what happens now?' I asked.

'Your guess is as good as mine,' Andy replied wearily. 'It was all we needed, wasn't it? Terry has put through a call to London and Pattison is flying out tomorrow for an on-the-spot conference. In the meantime, we're to send out a press notice that we're postponing for a week and the only thing is to wait and see. I suppose there's a faint chance of organising something in time for the New York opening, but I wouldn't rate it any higher.'

It struck me as a sad reflection on Hugo's life and character that Andy should now be demonstrating far less concern for his death than for the effect this would have on the play. It was true that he had not been a particularly endearing man, and that Andy was a director first and a human being second, but listening to him one would have assumed, and correctly no doubt, that he was not so much distressed by the violent end of a colleague as annoyed with him for being careless enough to get himself mugged and murdered only days before the scheduled opening.

I believe this reaction was shared by many of us and yet I found something in Detective Meek's report which did not quite fit the normal pattern of robbery with violence and which made me wonder if the crime had been quite so haphazard as it appeared; whether, in effect, we did not do Hugo an injustice in laying most of the blame at his own door.

'In the first place,' I remarked to Toby, who had also been inclined to dwell on the financial aspect, 'what about the hat?'

'What about which hat?'

'The one they found lying in the gutter beside Hugo. It was one of those tweedy things you see people wearing at horse shows in the *Tatler*.'

'Oh, was it? I wouldn't know, since I rarely got to horse shows in the Tatler, but I can see that it would be the kind of jest to appeal to that rather puerile mind. He was one of those dim personalities who drew confidence from the pretence of being grander than God made him. No doubt, he hoped to impress the mob by passing himself off as a limb of the British aristocracy.'

'Exactly, Toby! I call that a very shrewd assessment.'

'You sound triumphant,' he remarked gloomily, 'and although you try to flatter me, I suspect your congratulations are really for yourself. Why should that be, I wonder?'

'Because, if this should turn out to have been a pre-meditated crime and not the mindless affair that it appears, does it not strike you that Hugo may have been mistaken for someone else?'

'No, it doesn't, and I never heard such pernicious nonsense in my life. I quite see what you are driving at; that someone really meant to kill Gilbert and, while I can understand that such a notion would provide a lot of fun for you in these rather dull days, that, my dearest Tessa, is not quite what we're after.'

'You protest so much that I feel certain you have already had the same thought yourself.'

'If so, I should have repressed it immediately. I don't share your passion for mysteries. Mine is a practical nature and I am well aware that, whereas we may just manage to limp along with one member of the cast violently done to death, there would be no chance at all if someone else in the company were to be arrested for his murder. For that is where it would end, I must warn you. Furthermore, I find it quite laughable that you should base your fantastic theory on the single fact that the man was wearing a funny hat when he was attacked.'

'It is based on more than that,' I admitted.

'Then please don't say another word. I don't wish to hear.'

'I'm afraid you must, Toby, if I am really to put it out of my mind. Perhaps you will find some sensible argument to prove me wrong, but if I don't speak out it will hang between us like a sinister cloud.'

'Let it! I have no objection to sinister clouds, I rather like them.'

'No, you don't, otherwise you wouldn't be so alarmed at this moment.'

Toby sighed: 'I am not faintly alarmed, but if there is no other way to end this foolish argument I am prepared to admit defeat. So what else was suspicious about Hugo's death, apart from the fact that it occurred at all?'

'There speaks your subconscious! That is the whole answer. The extraordinary thing is that it occurred at all.'

'That is one way of describing it, but do you happen to have come upon any statistics relating to the number of people who get knocked off every week in this city?'

'Certainly, I do; people rarely talk about anything else. I've even had some personal experience, in so far as I probably only missed Lorraine's attacker by a few minutes. I also have a very knowledgeable source of information in Muriel, the cleaning lady, and according to her, the mugging victims don't normally end up dead. It's either robbery or murder and ninety percent of the murders come into the vendetta category, nothing whatever to do with the general public. She was saying this to cheer me up, actually, and she explained that if I was ever held up I must on no account scream or try to resist because so long as I handed over all my worldly goods I wouldn't get into any trouble. So I repeat: why was Hugo killed at all?'

'Not having benefited from Muriel's advice, presumably because he screamed or tried to resist.'

'No, that won't do, Toby. He was attacked from behind and you don't resist by turning your back on someone who's waving a knife.'

'Then perhaps the fellow was so incensed at having gone to all the trouble of waylaying one whose pockets looked to be lined with gold, only to find they contained nothing but his bus fare in a plastic purse, that he knifed him out of pure spite?'

I shook my head: 'I'm afraid that won't do either, because he certainly wouldn't have hung about while he counted up the loot. Obviously, in a hold up of that kind the first major priority, as they say in the vernacular, is to remove yourself from the scene with all speed.'

'Very well,' Toby said grimly, 'as you're so clever at tearing other people's arguments to shreds, here's one for you to stitch together again. I take it you have now convinced yourself that someone set out to murder Gilbert, for private, personal motives, and to make it look like any old twopenny halfpenny street robbery, but unluckily caught the wrong man?'

'Right!' I agreed. 'Correct in every detail.'

'Then you're out of your mind.'

'Why?'

'Because although he could conceivably have mixed up their identities at a distance, he'd have got all that sorted out as soon as he came within range. It is the height of absurdity to suggest that you could get within knifing distance of either of those two without recognising him for exactly who he was.'

'But supposing Hugo had turned round at that point and seen the knife? Then the murderer might have found it necessary to silence him.'

'You have just proved to my entire satisfaction that Hugo did not turn round.'

Although somewhat shaken by this argument, I was nevertheless reluctant to see my theory knocked out of the ring in the first round and made a determined effort to revive it:

'All right, but what if it was a hired assassin? Supposing someone had been paid to wait at the theatre every evening and then to follow Gilbert, and to keep on doing this until the opportunity came to kill him? If Gilbert had only been pointed out to him from a distance he might easily have been taken in by Hugo's impersonation. Presumably, people of that sort aren't terribly bright.'

'No, and people of your sort aren't always terribly bright either. The idea is really too far fetched for any words. Very tempting for you, naturally, when someone in your little circle has been done to death, to alleviate the boredom by finding ways and means to prove that someone else, equally close at hand, is responsible. I sympathise, but I must insist on your keeping it within those bounds. I really cannot have you handing it out to sub-contractors.'

Thoroughly squashed by this sarcasm, I did not refer to the subject again, though by no means ceasing to puzzle over it and the resulting uneasiness was not diminished by having to spend a night alone in Lorraine's house. In straining my ears to catch every creak and rustle which might presage a break in, I caught so many of them that there could have been a regiment of armed desperadoes positioned about the house before dawn broke and eventually, abandoning all hope of sleep, I got up and wrote a long letter to Robin. I described Hugo's death to him in some detail, adding that, in the event of his being unable to come over to America and sort things out for us, he should at least advise me how to proceed and whether to present all the facts to Detective Meek. In saying this, I was not really, as in Toby's unkind version, manufacturing dramas to relieve my own boredom; nor even furthering the cause of justice, American justice in the abstract representing an even more remote concept than the homegrown variety, but because I too had a stake in the play's future and did not rate its chances very high if the present trend were to continue unchecked.

If someone had in truth set out to murder Gilbert and had inadvertently picked the wrong man then, unless a spoke was inserted pretty smartly in his wheel, there was really nothing to prevent his trying again.

CHAPTER TWO

THE council of war was convened for the following evening, a few hours after the arrival of Mr Pattison from London. I was not a party to it, but the upshot was that an actor named Oliver Barton, who had made a corner in English parts on Broadway, had been engaged to join the company in Hugo's place, subject to a week's delay in which to complete a television spectacular. His dramatic interpretations were competent and also very nearly unique, for he had perfected an accent all his own, which had no roots in either country, with the result that most American audiences took him for an Englishman trying to speak American and everyone else assumed he was from outer space. However, he was a draw in his own backyard and it was agreed that it would be more practical to take him on than to start from scratch with a London actor, for whom the delicate negotiations for work permits, clearance with Equity and so on would have to be gone through all over again.

Hugo's remains were to be flown back to England for cremation, following a form of Memorial Service at the Embassy, after which the live members of the cast found themselves with one week out and nothing much to fill it. Gilbert immediately took off for Connecticut, accompanied by Harrison, and Toby invited me to go to New York with him. However, one week's break with about half of it spent in trains was not an alluring prospect, so I told him that, much as I appreciated the offer, my duty lay in Georgetown, nursing Lorraine back to health and strength, and I used the same excuse when Catherine, to my immense astonishment, graciously suggested my joining her and Rose on an expedition to Charlottesville. They were hiring a car and driving down for one night, in order to give Monticello a thorough going-over.

It was all rather tough on Lorraine, who appeared to be in the pink of health once more and might have been grateful for the chance to have Henry to herself for the weekend. Also I would have been glad to see Monticello myself, but driving with Catherine, even on roads where she felt at home, could be a nerve racking experience, in no way mitigated by the constant, querulous complaining of Rose. After twenty years of it she was still scared out of her wits, which had the disastrous effect of spurring Catherine on to even more reckless behaviour.

So, with two avenues of escape being closed to me, due to their unacceptable means of transport, I resolved to put the free time to good account and to do some penance for the lies I had told by applying myself resolutely to the task of writing overdue letters and postcards to England.

The prime necessities in such a programme were writing materials and stamps and the first was easy to come by, being on sale in every drug store and supermarket in a city where every second shop is either a drug store or a supermarket. Tracking down a post office was quite another matter, since in Washington they have a somewhat similar aura to golden eagles in Scotland; i.e. known to exist, seen by a privileged few and their exact location a closely guarded secret. However, Lorraine told me she had heard rumours of one having been sighted on Pennsylvania Avenue, not too far from H Street, and accordingly I set forth in search of it on Saturday morning. She was dead right too, and I found it after parading up and down for a mere twenty minutes; only, being Saturday, it was not open for business.

This was most dispiriting, so I crossed the road again, which took several more minutes, with all the signals switching inexorably to 'Don't Walk' each time I approached, and entered a bar I had noticed on earlier perambulations, hoping that a dry martini would revive me sufficiently for a fresh assault on the problem. It was called Toni's Bar and Restaurant Pizza Pizza Pizza and, so far as I could tell, through the dense, smoke-filled gloom, was packed from floor to ceiling with pizza addicts making an early start.

I sat down on the first available empty chair, having sought permission from the table's existing occupant, which he granted with a wave of the hand, without looking up from his newspaper. However, with the arrival of the waitress, a plump girl wearing a gingham dress over jeans and a mane of flaxen hair over that, he glanced up and revealed himself to be Detective Meek. A minute later he removed his reading glasses and recognised me as well, but in the meantime I had twice been on the point of getting up and gliding away, overcome by the absurd notion that he would imagine I had followed him there. Only the thought of the martini already twirling around in the ice kept me in my seat.

'Hi, there, Miss Crichton! Nice to see you!' he said with a nervous snort of laughter. 'You following me around, by any chance?'

'Of course not. What a ridiculous idea!'

'You're right,' he agreed with a hopeless sigh. 'Don't know what makes me say these things.'

'I was looking for a post office, as it happens.'

'Oh well, yes, naturally; that makes sense. How about a drink, since I can't sell you any stamps?'

'You're very kind, but I just ordered one.'

'Well, have two! No, no, take no notice! I mean, have the one you just ordered on me? Why not? I don't often get the chance to buy drinks for famous London actresses.'

'Thank you, but it's only fair to warn you that I'm not famous, in London or anywhere else.'

'To me, you are!' he said with another hoarse burst of laughter, as our orders arrived together, his consisting of a cup of milky coffee and a pile of salad on a banqueting dish.

'Aren't you eating?' he enquired, digging into this repulsive looking heap.

'No, I'll be lunching at home later on.'

'Where's home?'

'Georgetown. I'm staying with a friend who lives there.'

'Sure, you are! A Mrs Lorraine Beaseley. Swanky, eh?'

'Not a bit. She's a single woman of slender means. She got coshed the other day.'

'Too bad! Happens all the time, so they tell me. Where was this?'

'In her own house. Would that be on your beat?'

'My?'

'Area, division?'

'No, they have their own down there. More refined. Is that why you were following me around? To tell me about your friend?'

'But I wasn't. I didn't even know it was you until I sat down.'

'I know, I know. Have another of those?'

'No, thanks. This one has set me on my feet. I'll struggle on now and leave you to eat your lunch in peace.'

'Not if you go away, you won't.'

'Why's that?'

'Because I can't tell what the Freudians would say about you picking on this particular table, but I do know that ever since you sat down you've been figuring out whether to ask me something and I feel I have a right to know what it is. Put it down to instinct, if you like, but you have that look of someone with something on her mind. I can smell it a mile off.'

'Oh, in that case,' I said, sitting down again. 'It's not all that important, but I confess it did cross my mind to ask whether your local hoods normally knife someone in the back after they've mugged him.'

'It can happen,' Detective Meek replied as steadily as though this were the precise question he had been expecting.

'I realise it can happen because it did happen. The question was, how common is it?'

'You have to take into account there could be a diversity of factors here. The guy could have been in a hurry and having to make sure his victim was in no state to raise the alarm, if there happened to be a prowling car in the area, or even a group of pedestrians who might make trouble.'

'Yes, I understand all that, but why not just knock Hugo unconscious?'

'A knife would have been just as quick and a lot more permanent.'

'So you're quite satisfied?'

'Oh, me! I'm never satisfied, ask anyone! But there's not too much I can do about it. I don't have the authority, for one thing. In the case of some local guy getting himself murdered I could possibly make a few enquiries on the side; find out what kind of company he'd been keeping, whose wife he'd been visiting with recently, that kind of thing; but here I'd be walking on a tightrope and liable to break my neck if I tried it. What do I know about the background of one Mr Hugo Dunstan and how would I get to find out without stepping on a dozen powerful and sensitive toes?'

'Why not ask me? Mine are not all that sensitive.'

'So I noticed. And how come, is the question I've been asking myself? Here you are, virtually volunteering the information that one member of your team was responsible for the death of another, because that's what it amounts to, Miss Crichton. We haven't succeeded in turning up a single previous connection between the dead man and anyone in this country and he certainly hadn't formed any since he came here. If this was a deliberate killing it has to have been committed by one of your own bunch. There's just no other way you can look at it and you're bright enough to have seen that for yourself. Do you have positive evidence, or could this be just professional interest?'

'Why should you think so?'

'Oh, we checked on your private life, while we were at it, and I gather your husband is in the same line of business as myself. Don't tell me you've caught the bug too?'

'No, I haven't, but you're a bit contradictory, aren't you? A minute ago you were moaning about the impossibility of finding out about our backgrounds; now you calmly tell me you've not only checked on Hugo's social activities, but also on my domestic life. Not bad for someone who's supposed to be working with both hands tied behind his back. What else have you found out?'

'Nothing much. Nothing that your own Embassy couldn't turn up at ten minutes' notice and certainly nothing to give us the tiniest lead in the direction you've been pointing at. So I'd still be glad to hear if you have something positive, and if so, what?'

I considered this proposition, watching in some fascination as he scooped up the last shreds of his villainous looking green stuff, and then said:

'Since you couldn't or wouldn't act on it, I don't think I'll tell you.'

'No?' he enquired, picking up both checks and taking some bills from his pocket. 'Well, that's up to you, isn't it?'

He swivelled round to signal to the waitress and when their business was concluded I thanked him for the drink and he replied:

'My pleasure. What's your phone number, by the way?' He wrote it down, nodding approvingly: 'That's nice!'

'What's nice about it? It sounds very much like any other number to me.'

'No, I meant a straight answer; no evasions.'

'It would be a waste of time, would it not, Detective? You have made it perfectly clear that any evasions on my part would result in your finding the number all by yourself, in about two and a half seconds.'

'Oh, do call me Frank!' he said, patting my shoulder and uttering another terrible snort of laughter.

CHAPTER THREE

'YOUR car's back,' Lorraine called, waving to me from the top of the steps.

She looked as fresh as a daisy after forty-eight regular hours of what I was learning to call hospitalisation and the broad white bandage round her head, camouflaging the patch where she had been stitched up, had been prettified by a necklace strung round the top of it, whose pear shaped red pendant rested against the bandage just above the bridge of her nose, making her look like a Rajah in drag.

'And they've done a good job, by the look of it; very dashing!' I said, eyeing the M.G., now parked in its old home again, with a somewhat dubious expression.

'Want to try her out? We could take a ride down to Alexandria, eat some seafood and poke around some of those lovely old warehouses they have there.'

'Well, I'm not sure about that Lorraine. Wouldn't you be nervous?'

'Would I hell? The only person makes me nervous driving is myself. And you have to see Alexandria! It's our ancient, historic port. All of a hundred years old, for all I know.'

'Oh, goodness, is it really? Fancy that! How about the insurance, though? Would you be covered if someone banged into me?'

'No one's going to bang into you, honey. They all love you and they all want you to be happy. Now will you please, kindly stop making excuses and let's get started?'

'Oh, very well, but you'll have to hang on for a second while I go and dig out my international licence.'

The second was so far extended that anyone else might have concluded that I had jumped out of the window in sheer despair, but Lorraine possessed a remarkable ability to take life literally as it came, inch by inch and moment by moment, and when I finally emerged from my bedroom, looking, as I believed, grim, pale and determined enough to shake the stoutest heart, she had become so tangled up in the intricacies of the current étude that it was all completely lost on her.

The first part of the journey required every drop of concentration that I could give it, as we nosed our jerky way into Wisconsin Avenue, joined the line of east-bound traffic on M Street and swooped round the Lincoln Memorial in an interminable fashion, before I summoned the nerve to break out of the flow, to be thrown up at last on the comparatively peaceful shores of Route 95, well and truly Alexandria bound and not a single bone broken.

Elated by this achievement and full of quiet confidence now, I said:

'I suppose you haven't had any more total or partial recall about that mishap of yours, Lorraine?'

'No, only what I told you. Why?'

'And you really have no idea who the man could have been?'

'Not one. You have to watch it here, Tessa, because we need to make a left turn pretty soon and most of them are wrong-way. Try the next one after this.'

'You don't consider it possible, for instance, that although you've no memory of it now, it was actually someone you recognised and that's why you had no qualms about turning your back on him while you hitched up the bike?'

'No, I don't consider that possible in any shape, form or kind. I never for one moment suspected there was anyone there in the house. All I knew was that one minute I was opening my own front door and the next I was sitting up in my little white bed, with you and Henry goggling at me. Gosh, darn it!' she broke off, flinging herself with great zest into this self-parody, 'That could just be a parking space ahead of us! Behind that yellow one, see?'

I saw and dismissed it as useless, impractical and not large enough to accommodate a doll's pram, so Lorraine took over the wheel and, by doggedly zigzagging to and fro and holding up the traffic for miles back, eased us in at last, with three centimetres to spare at either end and only minimal damage to the yellow car.

Flushed with triumph, she next switched her energies to locating that one special restaurant where the crab was really fresh out of the sea, and which turned out to be down quite a different turning from the one memory had dictated, so it was a good fifteen minutes before I found myself gazing into my second martini of the day and heard her ask:

'So what's bugging you, anyway? Why does it have to be someone I know?'

'Because I'm stuck with the idea that he wasn't an ordinary burglar; not a professional, that is, and certainly not looking for the obvious things, like transistors and so on. There was plenty of that stuff in your living room and he ignored it and concentrated on the bedroom.'

'I know, I know, but that doesn't mean he wouldn't have gathered up those other things on his way out. No point in dragging them along while he had a look to see what other goodies might be there for the picking. We've been through all this a dozen times and Henry says . . .'

'I know what Henry says, but you see, Lorraine, he is not in full possession of the facts. For instance, did you find when you came home yesterday that your room was in a bit of a mess?'

'Nowhere near so bad as you described it.'

'That was because Muriel had been to work, but there'd been an odd sort of pattern about it, which was very obvious at the time. One half was a shambles, the other didn't look as though it had been touched.'

Lorraine clenched her fists and banged her knuckles against her forehead, then, discovering that this was still a tender spot, dropped her hands on the table and glowered at me from under the bandage.

'Listen, Tessa, you've got yourself all screwed up over this, you know. I realise it must have been a shock for you, coming from your nice little docile island, where everyone obeys the law and you don't have these hoods and housebreakers, but . . .'

'That's rot, Lorraine, as well you know!'

'Well, there has to be something to account for this obsession that it was off key in some way. You aren't thinking straight. Can't you see it's just how it would have happened if he'd been interrupted half-way through the job? He'd have heard me come in and after that there wouldn't have been any more time to search my room or pick up anything on his way out. All he would think about was getting the hell out.'

'So you and Henry have repeated, ad nauseam, but I've always considered there was something wonky about that theory. If he was in such a hurry, why did he choose to go out through the hall, where he was bound to run into you, instead of through the garden window, where he could have escaped with no trouble at all? It simply doesn't make sense, but quite apart from that I've now discovered something else.'

'In my bedroom?'

'No, in mine. Wasn't that strange? It never occurred to me that he'd been in there, because on the surface nothing had been moved.'

'It never occurred to me either. You mean to tell me something of yours is missing? Gosh, that's awful, Tessa! Now we really will have to tell the police.'

'No, hang on a minute, Lorraine. Nothing is missing.'

'No? Then what the hell is this all about?' she demanded.

'Something I discovered when I went up to fetch my driving licence just now. I keep it with a bundle of vital things, like travellers' cheques and passport and so on, in the zip pocket of my suitcase. This may sound completely crazy to you, but I'm fanatical about that sort of thing. It's a real fetish and I could probably tell you the exact order all those papers were arranged in.'

'All the same, if none of them is missing, so what? What's all the fuss about?'

'The point is that they'd been taken out of the zip compartment and strewn all over the bottom of my case, as though someone had sorted them in a hurry and hadn't stopped to put them back properly. Now, I know I would never have left them like that in a million years, you'll just have to take my word for it, and something tells me that Muriel is the last person to go snooping through other people's belongings.'

'You're so right,' Lorraine agreed. 'You could leave the Hope Diamond lying around for weeks and the most she would do would be to give it a good polish and put it back where she found it. So what are we supposed to make of this?'

'I don't know what you make of it, but it seems fairly clear to me that it wasn't anything of yours the thief was after, but something of mine, or at any rate something he believed I possessed, and it wouldn't have been a camera or transistor either.'

'What's your idea then?' Lorraine asked, frowning so fiercely that the crimson bauble dangled on to her nose.

'It looks to me as if he must have started in the smaller of the two bedrooms, believing it to be mine. That doesn't necessarily prove he was a stranger, let me add, because even one of your friends might not realise you were the kind of eccentric who kept the best room for the guests and took the other for herself.'

'Eccentric nothing! I just happen to prefer the little room. It's snug.'

'Nevertheless, that's not the usual way of it. Most people take the view that if anyone has to be snug it should be the visitor, and if this intruder had been looking for something of mine he would have gone automatically to your room and, since we're both female, with the usual number of limbs and buy our clothes from places all over the world, it might have taken him quite a while to grasp that he was in the wrong place. When it eventually dawned on him he bolted into the other bedroom. That, in my opinion, is the only logical explanation for the fact that one half of your room was turned upside down and the other half not touched and it would also help to explain why he left by the front entrance instead of out through the garden. In other words, Lorraine, he wasn't interrupted while he was on the job. He'd either completed it or given up. The chances are that he didn't hear you at all and it was just your bad luck that you happened to run into him; which makes everything worse than ever, in a way, because now I feel partly responsible.'

'Oh, pooh to that! It's a nice theory you've got there, but I'm not entirely persuaded. I can believe one part of it, that he began in my room before moving on to yours. That does make sense because it could account for his not having heard me; although you'd think he might have taken a few precautions before walking downstairs straight into my arms. And all the rest is pure supposition. The fact is, Tessa, you don't have too much experience of these shenanigans. You're assuming the hoods act in a rational, systematic way and I can tell you that's not how it is at all. Half the time they're so stoned or so desperate for a fix that they act more like zombies than people. Ask Henry, if you don't believe me. Personally, I'm perfectly clear what happened. We both had our rooms gone over and neither one of us has lost anything. So okay, he was looking for cash, or maybe the kind of jewellery or whatever he would know how to convert into cash. Nine houses out of ten on my street would probably have paid off, but they'd mostly have been a lot harder to break into. He chose the easy one. He was hoping for a quick snatch and he'd seen one of us pick up the key to let ourselves in, so it must have looked like a cinch. Only had to wait around until we'd both gone out and then swoop. It was his bad luck that it didn't bring results, but if anyone's to blame it's me, for being so damn cocky and careless with the key. I operated on the principle that if you had nothing worth stealing no one would bother to come looking for it, but it shows how wrong you can be. As of now, we'll be bolted and barred with the best of them and the only headache will be that we're so well protected neither one of us will be able to find our way in or out.'

It was difficult to gauge from her tone whether her object was to reassure me or convince herself, but either way it would have brought no comfort to have her argument blown to pieces, so I dropped it, symbolically setting aside the bowl of salad and glass of iced water with which the management had been kind enough to present me, and gave my full attention to the very special crab. It merited every bit of it too and yet, in a way, I felt cheated. Food and drink are all very fine, but what I most hungered for just then was a chance to develop my theory whereby a direct link could be traced between Lorraine's break-in and Hugo's murder.

CHAPTER FOUR

1

'CARE to drop by for a drink at my place this afternoon?' Detective Meek enquired in his brusque, rough-hewn fashion. 'Your friend too, if she wants.'

This was on Sunday morning, one of Muriel's nondays, when we had to make our own breakfast and answer the telephone single-handed. It was not a grave hardship because Lorraine's kitchen was equipped, in true American style, like a miniature, rustic factory, a dazzling combination of natural pine and high-powered technology, and the telephone was cheek by jowl with the coffee percolator and juice machine. Usually Lorraine got to it first, hoping to hear Henry's voice, which she invariably did, but on this occasion she happened to be in the shower.

'I can answer for my friend,' I said. 'She is heavily otherwise engaged.'

'Fine! How about answering for yourself?'

'It depends why you've invited me. Not to take my finger-prints, by any chance?'

'I might at that, but don't worry, they'll stay in my private collection. Today is Sunday and I'm inviting you for a drink, right?'

'Right. What time?'

'Around four-thirty suit you?'

My enthusiasm for this outing, never at fever pitch, dropped to zero at this point, but I reminded myself that a man accustomed to lunching before midday could well be thirsting for cocktails by four-thirty p.m. and furthermore, after twenty-four hours of Lorraine and Henry falling over themselves to rid me of any idea that I was de trop, every avenue of escape deserved serious consideration.

'Actually, that's my tea time,' I said.

'Okay, we'll have tea. You can show me how to make it.'

'Hold the line a minute while I find a pen to write down your address.'

'Hanging from a chain right beside your hand,' Lorraine said, coming into the kitchen at this point. 'Muriel's idea, like so much of the smooth running side of my life.'

When I had concluded the business and rung off she asked, with far too much overdone casualness for an ex-pro:

'Does that mean you have to work today?'

'Not work exactly, at least I hope not. That was my dear old Detective.'

'Don't tell me he was trying to date you?'

'And not only trying. I am committed to dropping by at his place at four-thirty this p.m.'

'Does he have a wife?'

'No mention of one. If he has, she doesn't know how to make tea.'

'Would you like Henry to drive you over there, or can you manage on your own now?'

'Oh, yes thanks, Lorraine. After all you put me through yesterday I could drive to Cincinnati on my own now. Anything fascinating in the papers?'

'Take your pick,' she replied, dropping the whole hundredweight of them on to the kitchen table.

I helped myself to the section sub-titled 'Theatre—Films—Art', Lorraine took 'Books—Décor—Social', with 'Scene—Places—Obituary' as a bet hedger, and Henry, joining us a few minutes later, fresh from the shower like a fragrant liquorice all-sorts in his striped towelling robe, whipped up the comics, which he proceeded to plough through with the utmost solemnity and, so far as I could detect, not the smallest tremor of amusement.

After a silence punctuated by the rustle of paper and clink of coffee cups, Lorraine said:

'They've given your friend, Hugo, quite a write-up.'

'Good! He'd have been pleased about that.'

'Want to read it?'

'Later. There's a piece about the play in this one. At least, it starts off with how the opening has been postponed, due to the tragic death, etcetera, and then it develops into a feature about thrice wed Gilbert Mann, forty-six . . . and there's a couple of understatements, to start with.'

'Well, at least he's alive to enjoy it.'

'The interviewer kicks off by asking if he's ever previously been involved in a major postponement situation, so perhaps we can forgive him for becoming a bit bemused.'

Henry glanced up momentarily with a puzzled frown and Lorraine said:

'How did he make out with that one?'

'Much as you'd expect, I gather, with many a rueful grin and quizzical upward shooting of the celebrated eyebrows. Also quite a lot about the wonderful empathy and response of American audiences.'

'That's funny,' Lorraine remarked absently.

'No, it's not. If he were giving the interview in Alaska he'd have a lot to say about the wonderful empathy and response of Eskimoes.'

'I'm not talking about that, I'm still with Hugo and it says here that he was formerly married to the Honourable Daphne Holden, daughter of British industrialist and racehorse owner. Could there be two Honourable Daphnes who married into theatrical circles?'

'Half a dozen probably, but our Daphne's father is called Lord Holden and there's less likely to be two of those.'

'Did you know she was Hugo's ex?'

'No, but she's always been stage struck, so I suppose it was a case of per ardua ad astra. And after going through all that it looks as though the poor girl is now about to lose her astra. However, it makes one think.' Once again Henry raised an enquiring face and it had not escaped me that it was some minutes since he had maintained the pretence of studying his comics and had switched most of his attention to our conversation. Considering the average male American's dedication to any involvement situation affecting Charlie Brown, I felt flattered and, more with the object of holding his interest than expressing my own, I said:

'You remember all that nonsense of the bogus telegram saying that Daphne was about to descend on us?'

They both nodded and I went on: 'Well, I've always believed that Hugo might have been at the bottom of that. Presumably, it was meant as a practical joke, so he was the obvious culprit, except for one big snag.'

'Why was he, and what snag?' Lorraine asked.

'Well, you see, he was a compulsive practical joker and the more complicated he could make it the bigger the kick. There was often an element of spite too, specially when he was using it as a means to get his own back. Gilbert never missed an opportunity to snub him and although Hugo put on a brave show of taking it in good part you could see that it rankled. Sending Gilbert out on a wild goose chase and causing him to wait around in the small hours at Dulles Airport would have been a marvellous revenge. I thought so from the beginning, but unfortunately I could also see the fatal flaw. Hugo was too mean for a prank like that. The telegram itself wasn't a fake, so it would have cost him money to set it up and that would have ruled it out.'

'Well now, I don't see why that should necessarily be so,' Henry said, obligingly entering into the spirit of the thing by putting his finger tips together and speaking in a weighty, judicial manner. 'The way I see it, he would have needed an accomplice in any case, so why not have asked some chum in London to look after that end for him and then conveniently forget all about paying him back?'

'Yes, he'd have managed that part easily enough,' I agreed. 'No one better; but he still had to get in touch with this accomplice, didn't he? There wouldn't have been time for a letter and anyway he was probably too canny to put that sort of request in writing. I doubt if he would even have risked a cable. What it essentially needed was a telephone call and I just can't see Hugo lashing out to that extent. Unless, of course, he could find some way to reverse the charges.'

'Or maybe the call itself was reversed, how about that? Suppose it was all instigated by someone on the London end?'

'Like the Honourable Daph, for instance?'

'Right. Let's say she'd heard rumours about his love life and calls Hugo to check it out with him. Then when she hears it's true they hatch up this plot together.'

'Yes, that's good, Henry; well done! So Daphne having done her part, Hugo tips off the reporters that she's on her way over, whereupon Gilbert toddles off to meet her and gets egg all over his face, and his new girl friend is probably not overjoyed to learn that he's been hanging around at the airport half the night, waiting for Daphne. Very neat, and they must have been falling about with laughter to see it work out so beautifully. Poor old Hugo, he didn't have very long to enjoy it.'

'And that might not be pure coincidence either,' Henry suggested, really getting carried away now. 'Did you consider that angle?'

'No, I can't say I did. Are you implying that he was killed on account of some slightly malicious practical joke?'

'Not me, no. I believe he was killed by some hood for his pocket book and watch, but since you evidently don't, I'm surprised you haven't already come up with this as a motive. What's wrong with postulating that Gilbert knew his wife and her ex were still on friendly terms and was fully capable of working out who sent that cable, just as we have?'

'Nothing, I suppose, but it doesn't make him a murderer. Gilbert is far too shrewd to risk his own skin.'

'Not even for the charms of a multi-millionairess?'

'No, not even for them. I daresay he'd have left no stone unturned to get Hugo sacked and dragged down in the dust, but murder, no; not in a million years. Funnily enough, it's my belief that there was another practical joke connected with Hugo's death, quite different from the first and he can't have had any inkling of the danger it would put him in.'

Given any encouragement, I was prepared to enlarge on this theme and Henry was responding with gratifying, semi-serious attention to every word, but before I could get going Lorraine let out a yelp of astonishment and dropped her section of the newspaper on to the table as though it had stung her.

'What do you know? Karen Jones has written a book! Well, of all things! I didn't even know she could read!'

'I didn't even know she existed,' Henry admitted. 'Who is Karen Jones?'

'Oh, you must remember Karen Jones!'

'I am sorry, Lorraine, but I don't.'

'Yes, you do too, you met her in New York only a couple of months back. She was at the Delmont party. Tall, blonde, loud-mouthed female.'

'Well, that narrows it, I suppose, but not too much. There were several dozen there who fit that description. What's so wonderful about her writing a book?'

'Just that she's the last person in the world who I would ever expect to put pen to paper.'

'Life is full of surprises,' Henry remarked, not sounding as though this one would materially influence the statistics.

'I'm surprised you don't remember Karen Jones, that's the real surprise,' Lorraine said mulishly, which only went to show that what Henry said was perfectly true and what most surprised me was that she should persist in floundering on with this perfectly pointless subject in the face of such overt indifference. However, I assumed there must be some purpose in it, so obligingly offered a hand by enquiring what the book was about.

'Oh, how would I know that? Herself, I guess. Any book that Karen wrote would have to be about herself.'

So there it was and it had been such a lame excuse to turn our thoughts away from Hugo's death that evidently the need to change the subject had been paramount to all other considerations. I could think of only one reason for this and it constituted the biggest surprise of all. It was almost unbelievable that Lorraine should have been piqued by my engaging Henry's interest for five minutes, for she was the least jealous or possessive woman I knew. Nevertheless, the signposts were clear enough to banish any lingering doubts I might have had about keeping my appointment that afternoon with Detective Meek.

2

In asserting that I now felt capable of driving the M.G. to Cincinnati, should the need arise, I had picked this name out of the blue, having only the vaguest notion of its geographical location, simply because it was the most remote and unlikely destination that occurred to me, although as it happened Detective Meek's apartment could just as well have been in that city, instead of a dozen blocks east of Georgetown, for all it had in common with other homes I had seen in Washington. It was neither sleek and luxurious like Catherine's, nor quaint and elegant in the colonial style, having evidently been constructed between these two periods, out of hideous blood red brick and reflecting a strong Swiss architectural influence.

It comprised an upper storey in one of a row of eight terraced houses, all bow fronted and those at each end being adorned by a tall, top-heavy looking turret with a pointed gothic roof. The interior of these would doubtless have afforded spectacular views over the city and they were quite large enough to be used as rooms, but to all appearances were not inhabited and indeed several of the houses looked empty and neglected as well, with grimy, broken window panes, wads of newspaper wedged into the crevices between the sills and the brickwork and piles of mouldering rubbish littering the steps and desolate little front gardens.

There was no lift and the stairs were uncarpeted, reviving memories of my agent's office in Soho, but all similarity ended there, for this living room was extremely neat and clean, in a drab kind of way, with not a single dirty coffee cup in sight.

Two other guests had arrived before me, a youngish couple named Bob and Estelle Mason, whose greeting was almost alarmingly effusive and hearty. I had formed no pre-conceived notions as to why I had been invited, preferring to enjoy the mystery for as long as possible, but a forced element in their cheerfulness, combined with Detective Meek's patent, throat clearing embarrassment, conveyed the hint that, whatever the reason, he had subsequently lost faith in it and the Masons had been dragged in for no better purpose than set dressing, in an eleventh hour attempt to present this as an ordinary social occasion.

This pretence was not helped by my arriving twenty minutes late, having even on a dead Sunday afternoon run into all the usual parking difficulties, for it immediately became clear that the Masons had already used up most of the time they had allotted for this gesture. The introductions were scarcely completed before Bob started looking at his watch and outdoing the Detective in the throat clearing contest, and Estelle gravely explained to me that they just hated to run away, but were due to collect their elder child from a barbecue in outer Virginia, after which they had promised to drop by on Bob's mother, who was not in terribly good shape these days and had arthritis problems, before collecting the baby sitter in time to get back home and change to go out for dinner with a business colleague of Bob's. By the time she had finished this catalogue I felt tired out just thinking about it and so depressed by my own comparative lethargy that I gratefully accepted Detective Meek's offer to fix me a bloody mary. Taking this as a signal that the ball had started to roll and no further throws were required from their side, both Masons jumped up with superb co-ordination, saying how nice it had been to meet me, before speeding on winged feet to the door.

The host followed them into the lobby, perhaps with some half hearted idea of entreating them in sign language to relent, but if so the mission failed because shortly afterwards the front door slammed and he reappeared on his own, muttering something about fetching more ice from the frigidaire.

Feeling as silly and superfluous as a forgotten poached egg, I picked up a brown folder from the butcher's block coffee table and saw that it was labelled 'Deputy Medical Examiner's Report', followed by the previous day's date and half a dozen code numbers. In my hard up state, I should probably have opened it in any case, but the fact that the label also bore the words 'Private and Confidential' and the name Dunstan H, in brackets, was enough to clinch it.

Detective Meek must have wrapped the ice cubes in flannel, for there wasn't so much as a clink of warning and the first intimation that he was back in the room came with his saying:

'Make anything of that?'

'Not very much,' I replied, deciding to brazen it out. 'Did you invite me here so that I could read it?'

'That was one reason,' he admitted with one of his wild snorts of amusement.

'What was the other?'

'So you could meet Bob and Estelle.'

'Oh, I see! Well, now that both have been accomplished, would you like me to leave?'

'I'd rather hear what you were able to pick up from that report.'

'It all seems fairly negative. This knife, for instance: I imagine it was a pretty common sort of weapon?'

'Oh, sure! Pick one up anywhere.'

'And that must make it hard for you? I mean, no help in tracing the murderer and he didn't need to dispose of it?'

'Right!'

'So all you can say positively is that he was probably right handed and unlikely to have been either a midget or a giant?'

'That's about it.'

'Just another unpremeditated, unsolved, written off murder?'

'You said that, I didn't.'

'But Detective . . .'

'My name is Franklin, incidentally, and my few friends normally call me Frank. Now that you've eaten my salt, not to mention my pepper, tomato juice, Worcestershire sauce and vodka, couldn't we relax the British formality?'

'Okay, but what's wrong with Franklin? It's more distinguished.'

'Dates me. I don't want to be labelled all through my life as a New Deal baby.'

I made a quick reckoning, bringing him out at forty, or thereabouts.

'Forty-two,' he said, grinning at me. 'See what I mean?'

'All right, Frank it is; and tell me, Frank, since you can't even make guesses about the age, colour, sex or height of the assassin, how could you possibly ever hope to identify him?'

'It's minimal, I agree. The only chance we would have is by attacking the problem from another angle, which is where you come in, Tessa. And that reminds me: why aren't you called Theresa?'

'Because so many people, starting with you, rhyme it with freezer.'

'What's wrong with that?'

'I'd rather stick to Tessa, if you don't mind. What did you mean by saying that was where I came in?'

'Where you already are in, to be exact. Something you let drop the other day was what set me off on this whole thing; which I want you to know is an activity strictly confined to my leisure,' he added, finding another rhyme for Theresa. 'Officially, like you said, the case will be filed under unsolved homicide.'

'So why bother?'

'Don't know that I can explain it, Tessa. I suppose you could call crime my hobby, as well as my job, but there's more to it than that. It kind of sticks in my gullet that somebody should get away with it. It's bad enough with these city hoodlums we have to deal with every day of our lives, but at least you could argue they didn't have much chance to grow up any other way. Violence is about the only skill they've learnt; but killing in cold blood by someone who's been born with all the privileges, that's something else. If there was a chance of this being one of those I'd be happy to catch up with him if I could.'

'And how did I give you the idea that it might be?'

'You don't remember? It was when you asked me whether the victim normally got slain in a hold-up. It wasn't just the question either. There was something about the way you asked it which indicated more than a general curiosity. This is my weekend off and after I left you I went to a movie. It was some dopey thing about a private eye in L.A., but I couldn't tell you any one thing that happened. I found I just wasn't concentrating. Too busy trying to work out why you'd said that and what I intended to do about it.'

'And what do you intend to do about it?'

'The question is, what are we both going to do about it? I wouldn't get to first base on my own, but you're in a different situation. You know these people inside out. You've worked with them, lived with them; you know about their domestic problems; their loves, hates, prejudices; you . . .'

It was turning into an oration to the War Veterans and time to interrupt:

'It doesn't follow that I'd be willing to share the knowledge, specially if it meant landing one of them in the soup. We have our loyalties in my profession, I must remind you; quite famous for them, in fact.'

'I know, I know. I'm probably taking too much for granted, and jumping to conclusions that don't exist, but you do have two loyalties, Tessa. As I understand it, this wouldn't be the first time you'd been instrumental in helping to solve a killing?'

'Oh yes, I keep forgetting you've got all our dossiers. Quite a thorough job you've made, by the sound of it. Which suggests that any help I could give would be rather superfluous.'

'Wrong. All I've gathered is facts. They can be useful when you're dealing with professionals. Quite a help sometimes to know that the man you're interrogating has been indicted for a similar crime in the past, but facts of that nature aren't likely to be very plentiful here. Okay, okay, let's forget it, if that's what you want. It was probably a crazy idea in the first place and I suppose I have to be out of my mind to go looking for trouble when I have more than I can handle already. Maybe you should have had a dry martini, though?'

'No thanks, this is fine.'

'More inhibiting, I guess. Did I dream it, or was that a martini you were drinking yesterday, and did you or did you not throw out a hint the size of a brick that this might not be quite the simple, straightforward crime it looked to be?'

'True,' I admitted, 'but a hint was all it was. Not even that, really; more of a ruse to get you to reveal whether you were still working on it; certainly not an invitation to drag me in.'

'I am still working on it. In my own head, that is.'

'You must have a reason; apart from that rather nebulous one you've mentioned?'

'I do. Two, I guess. Number one the same as yours, that the robbery victim normally stays alive, unless he puts up a fight and has to be kept quiet, which doesn't appear to have happened here. Maybe I shouldn't tell you about the other one, if you don't care to be personally involved.'

'Would it personally involve me to hear it?'

'Only if you felt like providing some information.'

'Go ahead then! I can always refuse to answer.'

'It concerns a hat.'

'There now!'

'A man's hat, brand new, which was found within feet of the corpse. There's some pretty funny headgear walking around this city, but this was something else. Green and brown checks. I can only remember seeing one other like it and that was in a photograph.'

'Ah!'

'No surprises, so far?'

'No, I'd heard about the hat and I can guess whose head it was adorning in the photograph. Have you traced it to him?'

'If the question refers to Gilbert Mann, the answer is no. What we have done is trace it back to the shop where it was bought. It was one of those establishments in Georgetown where they specialise in phoney military gear, Gestapo uniforms, all that. They get quite a crowd in there, mostly young and mostly just gawping, but they have quite a brisk turnover too and neither sales clerk remembers who bought this particular hat. Only certainty is that it was a cash sale, not charge account. Any comments?'

'No, but I can hazard a guess.'

'Go ahead and hazard one.'

'One thing you should know about Hugo is that he was great on practical jokes. He really worked at it, going to immense pains to bring off elaborate, sometimes rather cruel tricks. I don't know why it had got such a hold on him,

but perhaps he was fundamentally a cowardly man and this
was one way he'd perfected of getting his own back. It often
gave his victims a nasty moment or two, but at the same
time there was a pretence that it was all just a merry lark
and they would be very stuffy and pompous to take offence.
Another thing it might be useful for you to know was that
he'd had to take quite a lot from Gilbert these last few days.'

'Would I be correct in stating that this applies to most
of the people in your company?'

'I suppose so, if you exclude Miss Fuller and Miss
Henneky. Catherine, Miss Fuller that is, is far too big a star
to be vulnerable. She's rated well above him in the profession and he wouldn't dare cross swords with her openly.'

'And Miss Henneky? She's the understudy, right?'

'Yes, and with her it's the exact reverse. She's meek and
unassuming by nature and too far down in the hierarchy to
be a worthy target. So far as one call tell, Gilbert thinks so
little of her that he wouldn't even bother to be rude.'

'He might have shown his contempt openly?'

'Not without putting himself on the wrong foot with
Miss Fuller.'

'That so? Well, go on, how about the rest of you?'

'The rest of us, including technicians, all got a pasting
from time to time, but on the whole I'd say we took it in
our stride. Hugo was the exception. He was the kind who
stores up grievances and works out complicated methods
of revenge.'

'And how would this impersonation game have helped
him there?'

'I can think of several ways. If he had gone into a bar
or some public place and had started a row or pretended
to be drunk or something like that, and there was no one
there who actually knew Gilbert personally, it could have
caused him a lot of embarrassment when the story got

around. Are you priding yourself on tricking me into being so frank, Frank?'

'Why, frankly no, Tessa, since all the insight I've gotten so far relates to the victim.'

'Yes, and whether you'll find it helpful or not I can't say, but there's another thing I may as well tell you before we leave the subject. On the day of his death he never came near the theatre at all and no one has ever discovered why.'

'I knew that too, but since you've brought it up I imagine you have some theory to account for it?'

'Only one. You'll remember my telling you that he was a great practical joker? Well, this time I think it may have been a case of turning the tables.'

Frank digested this information, along with a handful of nuts, which he tossed into his mouth from an exaggerated height, as though performing both parts in a circus act, a trick which I was already associating with keen cerebral activity. When the last nut had found its target he said:

'Who would want to do a thing like that?'

'No idea, and I might not tell you if I had.'

'Could that kind of absenteeism endanger his job?'

'Not if it were just an isolated case, but it could make him very unpopular.'

'Or somebody could have wanted him out of the way just on that one day? Does that make sense?'

'Not to me, and it may not even be relevant. Presumably, what really concerns us is whether he was killed deliberately or whether he got hoist with his own petard and the murderer mistook him for Gilbert; and I can't see how we'll ever find the answer to that one.'

'Yes, I know,' he said, dropping in another consignment of nuts. 'Might not be a bad idea to try, though, prevention being better than cure.'

My own brain might have worked faster if I had given it the nut routine, but it remained a blank.

'You and your loyalty!' he said with a heavy snort. 'Which side is it on now? Saving the skin of one of your team who may be a murderer, or helping to protect the life of your big star?'

CHAPTER FIVE

1

THE protection of Gilbert Mann had not hitherto figured prominently among my missions in life and it took some minutes to adjust to the role. Having partially succeeded, the programme underwent a major setback when Robin telephoned from London late on Sunday evening. Lorraine informed me that he had called twice while I was out visiting with Detective Meek and it may have been this frustration, combined with the fact that when he did succeed in establishing contact it was well past his bedtime, which made him unusually tetchy. The news of Hugo's death had been widely reported in England, in addition to which my own letter had just reached him and he had no doubt spent the intervals between abortive telephone calls picturing me undergoing the same treatment and lying dead on the sidewalk.

He calmed down a little when I told him about the loan of the M.G., which only necessitated exposing myself to the dangers of the public highway during the thirty seconds dash from her front door to the kerb, but the text of his sermon continued to be one of extreme caution and it was not the moment to remind him that Lorraine had been coshed practically on the spot where I was then standing, although it is conceivable that things might never have come to such a pass had I done so.

*

Rehearsals were resumed on Monday morning and the company, now brought back to strength by the arrival of our substitute from New York, reassembled at the Eisenhower at ten o'clock. Mindful of the conflicting instructions of my two police officers, I resolved to aim for some form of compromise, whereby to remain permanently on the alert for any suspicious word or gesture, but not to pass on any findings unless they proclaimed clear evidence of guilt, all of which signalled a fairly easy passage.

The first person I ran into was Marty Jackson, whose name has cropped up several times in this narrative, but who has not hitherto appeared in person and was destined to leave it again almost at once, since he informed me that he was catching the evening flight to London. I must have looked reproachful because he said defensively:

'Not my fault if the schedule gets gummed up, is it? I tried to explain about the postponement, but the firm I work for didn't want to know. They've booked me in for a three-day job in Manchester and I'm due in Melbourne the weekend after, so there's just no way I could stay on here, even if I wanted to, which I have to say I don't.'

'Yes, I see all that, Marty, but what about us? First they tell us we can't be heard further than the fifth row and now we're all going to look like blobs of ink, I suppose? It's the last straw.'

'Not to worry, love. I've got these boys trained now and they'll do a good job, I promise you. And I'll be back for the New York opening, which is what matters.'

'If we ever get there, Marty. It begins to look less and less probable. And have you noticed the pattern which is now beginning to emerge?'

'Yah, pattern of doom, you could say. Honestly, I'll be thankful to be out of it. Anyway, I must run now, got to pack and pick up some presents for the kids and all that. Bye, Tessa love, see you!'

'Bye, Marty, have a good trip!'

'Take care!' he called in the most uncaring way imaginable, as I walked towards the elevator.

If his indifference to our plight had been only a fraction more thickly veiled, I might have tried out my newest theory on him, for it had struck me while he was speaking that the most immediate impact of our various catastrophes was that, bit by bit, the production was falling into American hands. We already had a local lad about to step into one of the secondary roles, another poised to take over the company management, and now the lighting department, one of the key features from the actors' point of view, was about to go the same way. It even crossed my mind as I slid down to the lower floor that it was all the work of some disgruntled, unemployed actor, or hired agent of American Equity. The idea, though distinctly far fetched, was not quite so preposterous as it may sound. The British Theatre had virtually taken over Broadway that season and out of a dozen or so current smash hits all but two, and both of those musicals, had been imported, lock, stock, barrel and cast, from London. It was no exaggeration to say that there were several people who were a little put out by this, in every sense of the phrase.

However, I did not bother to expound the theory during my next encounter, which was with Jackie, despite the fact that coincidentally she provided me with another handful of fuel for its fires. She had come into my room for a bit of a chat while I unpacked a basketful of objects which I had put together over the weekend for the purpose of cheering up these rather austere surroundings and which included a bunch of dispirited roses from Lorraine's garden, and one look at her had brought the news that Time, the Great

Healer, had been at work and found a weekend to be quite sufficient for the purpose. She was once more the radiant bride and described to me at some length how she and Clive had drawn closer together in the face of genuine tragedy, instinctively turning to each other for comfort and realising in a flash that life was too short, etcetera, etcetera. Obviously, so far as her love life was concerned, Hugo had not died in vain, but I deduced that her recovery had been hastened by the fact that Gilbert had also been brought up with something of a jolt, with the result that the Don Juan of the Boards act had been temporarily dropped from the repertoire.

'Heard about Rose?' she enquired, when the earlier topic had been wrung dry.

'No. What about Rose?' I asked in some alarm.

'Fell down some steps and broke her ankle.'

'Oh really? How rotten! Still, I suppose they wouldn't ship her back to England on that account?'

'Ship her back to England? Are you barmy? I said her ankle, not her neck, for God's sake!'

'Yes, I know. Where did it happen? Clambering about on Monticello?'

'No, outside their apartment. She never got to Monticello.'

'And don't tell me Katie went without her, I couldn't bear it.'

'Why not?' Jackie asked, absently prodding at one of the roses which had abandoned the struggle to stay upright and was weeping quietly over the dressing table.

'Because it would be so odd and unsettling, and I've had enough. I'd like everyone to start behaving normally again.'

'Well, brace yourself, darling, because Catherine did go without her. Some plushy magazine had arranged to get photographs of her, gazing in rapture at Washington's bed, or whoever it was.'

'Jefferson. Well, that's not so bad. The job comes first, one can accept that.'

'And I expect it made a nice change for Rose to be on her own for a bit, don't you, duckie?'

'No idea,' I replied stuffily. 'No concern of mine.'

'Well, I'm the earthy type and I must confess that whole set up does rather fascinate me. You know what?'

'No.'

'I think half the time these migraines come from the nervous strain of having Katie clucking and fussing over her from dawn till dusk; and the rest of the time she invents them, just to get a bit of peace.'

This was disquieting, not because it gave open expression to a reality which I imagine was fairly widely understood, but for the discovery that Jackie was capable of wrenching her mind away from herself long enough to form any sort of opinion about another human being. After puzzling over it for about half a minute I regretfully came to the conclusion that someone had been gossiping to her, in which case it would not be long before these tidings came to Catherine's ears, with results which no one could foresee, but which would be unlikely to improve our somewhat shaky team spirit. Jackie was darting sly looks at me, which more or less confirmed these misgivings and I said:

'What put that idea into your pretty little head?'

Her answer was even more disturbing than the one I had first thought of, for she said, with a sweet, girlish smile:

'Well, actually, Rose did.'

'You amaze me, Jackie! You mean that Rose personally confided to you that Catherine got on her nerves?'

'Oh God, no, you must be joking! Madam Priss and I are not on those terms. The fact is, she disapproves of me madly, silly, bitten up, jealous cow.'

'Then how come?'

'I wouldn't pass this on to anyone except you, Tessa, but I know you're like the grave, and I think I've really sussed old Rosie. It happened that evening last week, after Clive and I had our silly row. It was idiotic, I know, but I was furious with him for banging out like that and leaving me flat. Of course I can see now that the poor love was so mis that he'd gone into a complete daze and hardly knew what he was doing.'

'And he met Rose on his wanderings?'

'No, nothing like that. At least, if so, he didn't mention it and I don't suppose he'd have recognised her if she'd come up and whacked him over the head with her umbrella, he was in such a tizz, poor lamb.'

'So what is this all about?'

'Well, you remember my telling you I meant to spend the whole afternoon in my dressing room? I really did mean to do just that too, only in the end I became so frantically bored and lonely that I just couldn't stick it a minute longer. I didn't want to go back to our hotel and risk running into Clive, so I decided to take a trip down to those boutiques on the corner block of the Watergate and buy some flash little outfit to cheer myself up. You know where I mean?'

'Yes, I get cheered up in them myself, from time to time.'

'Well, it must have been about five, I suppose, but that didn't matter because most of them stay open until far into the night, so there wasn't any rush, but you know how it is, Tessa? On the rare occasions when you do have time and money to spare and are absolutely set on buying something, it nearly always turns out there's simply nothing that really grabs you.'

'Yes, I do know, but what's all this got to do with Rose?'

'I'm coming to that, but you must let me tell it in my own way. After I'd been traipsing around for ages and trying on dozens of things, I began to feel so utterly exhausted and depressed that I was simply gasping for some quiet place to sit down in and I made up my mind to try and find my way through to the hotel.'

'Oh yes?'

'Don't say, "Oh Yes?" in that prissy tone! I know perfectly well what you're thinking and you're utterly and entirely wrong. I never gave Gilbert a thought and I certainly hadn't the faintest intention of going up to his room. All I wanted was a quiet place and a cold drink, only it was getting dark outside and I thought that easily the best thing would be to find a way through to the hotel and afterwards I could pick up a cab without any bother.'

'There is a way, as it happens.'

'I know. Someone pointed it out to me. It's a kind of subterranean passage, with telephone booths all down one side, and you know what, Tessa? You'll never guess who I saw crouched very furtively inside one of them.'

'Yes, I will; we had to get to Rose at some point and presumably it's here, but I still don't understand, what's so sensational about it. Her apartment is right across the street from there and, if she had felt the urge to cheer herself up too, it would have been the obvious place to pick. Having got there, one assumes that she then found it desirable to make a telephone call.'

Jackie sighed: 'You've missed the whole point, darling.'

'Yes, I thought I must have.'

'Don't you remember? That was the day when she was supposed to be flat on her back with the dreaded migraine? She didn't show up at the theatre at all in the morning and, later on, when she and Catherine were out shopping, she had to rush away and be sick in the powder room, or something.'

'Oh, was that the day?'

'That was the day all right,' Jackie said, nodding her head sagely and at the same time opening her bag to produce a little red velvet box containing a set of pearl earrings. 'What do you think of these, Tess? Clive gave them to me as a making-up present after our row. Wasn't it angelic of him? I don't normally very often wear earrings, but these are so super they've quite turned me on and I'm seriously considering getting my ears pierced. I don't know though . . . what do you think?'

I, too, expressed some doubts on the subject, though not those which chiefly beset me, for I was far from convinced that Jackie was so inconsequential and ingenuous as she would have me believe. It was just possible that she had been acute enough to drop the topic of Rose's duplicity at that point and allow me to add the final chapter off my own bat. Neither of us had alluded to the fact that all this had occurred not so very long before Hugo was found on a sidewalk only three blocks away from the Watergate, with a knife in his back.

2

'You see, if Gilbert had put it into her head that the migraines were psychosomatic, or even bogus, she could easily have used that as the basis for inventing the whole story about Rose,' I remarked thoughtfully. 'One should remember that Clive was also out and unaccounted for on the night Hugo was killed and, now that they're back in each other's arms, she may well be seeking to protect him by casting the net of suspicion a bit wider. It's usually a bad sign when people come up with some incriminating story about another person which can't be corroborated. More often than not an indication of the shakiness of their own position.'

'I expect you're right, but you go too fast for me,' Toby complained. 'Let us take this step by step. Why should Gilbert bother to put such a boring idea into her head?'

'Pure, innocent spite, I daresay, but obviously someone did. Jackie is not a complete fool, but she's indifferent to everything which doesn't affect her personally. Knowing what a talent Gilbert has for mixing it and also that she was inching her way into bed with him at that point and drinking in his every word, it seems logical. Of course, I may be doing him an injustice, but Lorraine told me rather a nasty story the other day, which has certain parallels with this one.'

'About a sham migraine?'

'No, not as close as that, but similar to it. This was about someone with a perfectly genuine illness, but with no visible symptoms to prove it, and Gilbert put it around that this person was an alcoholic. Not just for laughs either; he had a perfectly straightforward, selfish motive for spreading the story, though I can't see how that would apply in Rose's case, or how it would benefit him to drive a wedge between her and Catherine.'

'Neither can I and I've never met anyone like you for creating instant oaks out of acorns. Moreover, if your pathetic little tale about the maligned invalid refers to Lorraine herself, your sympathy is misplaced. She was a celebrated drunk at one point in her crowded life.'

'There you are, you see, Toby, you've exactly proved my point!'

'Then I can only say that your point must have shifted a little since you first made it.'

'No, you don't understand. That kind of slander always sticks and the fact that you've come trotting out with it about twenty years on simply shows what an expert Gilbert is.'

'No, it doesn't. There are two sides to this story and you have only heard one of them. Naturally, you accept Lorraine's version, quite right and proper, and I should be the first to hope that she could live it down after all this time, specially as I understand she is now about to marry into one of the stuffiest families in the land; but the fact remains that you were only a tot when she was on the rampage, whereas I was in my jaded twenties and can be expected to know what I am talking about. Not that I hope to convince you, I'm not insane, so let us pass on to the question of why you think little Jackie is trying to lay false trails in order to protect little Clive. Is there a rumour that he will be accused of murdering Hugo?'

'I doubt if anyone will be accused of it. I happen to know that the police are ready to give up, but I suppose it doesn't follow that the rest of us can dismiss it so easily; and in some ways it might be harder to live in the shadow of suspicion than to be called upon to defend oneself. After all, Clive was wandering around on his own that evening and people are bound to have taken note of the fact.'

'I see no reason why they should. There was no ill feeling between him and Hugo, was there?'

'Not as far as I know, but there was any amount of it between him and Gilbert. Things had really been stirred up that evening too, which is doubtless giving Jackie some bad dreams now.'

'Then she can sleep peacefully,' Toby declared firmly. 'Clive has nothing whatever to worry about.'

'Even though Gilbert was busily chasing his wife and Jackie was responding with enthusiasm, to the extent that she and Clive had just had a tremendous row about it?'

'You must know very well that it was nothing more than a game, with all three of them working it up into a great big drama, out of sheer boredom and frustration. I don't take it at all seriously and I feel sure that in their heart of hearts neither did they. However, that's not the point. It's this extraordinary idea you cling to, that Hugo was killed in mistake for Gilbert, which I feel it my duty to disabuse you of.'

'Let's see you try!'

'I grant you that someone who had never met either of them, but who knew Gilbert by sight as a big star bulging with money, might have been fooled by the disguise, but that brings us back to the premise that it was just an ordinary street hold-up. It is quite inconceivable that anyone who knew either of them well enough to have a motive for murder could have been taken in for one minute. You can have it whichever way you please, but not both.'

'Why not? Hugo was a fantastic mimic.'

'Come now, Tessa, you know better than that! I admit his talent lay in that line more than another, but like all impersonators he did it with a combination of tricks, the most important being his voice. If you'd heard him doing one of his acts while you were blindfolded it might have fooled you, but not otherwise, and certainly not if he was depending solely on mime. He was several inches shorter than Gilbert and several inches broader. The illusion of resemblance was sheer conjury and he could never have got away with it simply by putting on a funny Gilbert hat and ambling along in a funny Gilbert walk. Added to which, anyone who knew the first thing about Gilbert would be on their guard at once if they saw him moving from one point to another in anything except a funny Cadillac.'

'I wonder . . .' I said slowly. 'I just wonder . . . ?'

'Then you're a silly goat and I am sorry to have wasted my time.'

'You shouldn't be because I am deeply impressed by your argument. In fact, you've pretty well convinced me. It was your mention of the hat which did it.'

'Did what?'

'It's the only tangible evidence, isn't it? It was found on the scene of the crime, lying in the road beside Hugo. It was new and very similar to one which Gilbert often wore. That's all we know for certain. All the rest is guesswork.'

'All what rest?'

'The assumption that Hugo was wearing it for the purpose of passing himself off to the fans as Gilbert. Supposing he didn't do anything of the kind?'

'Idiotic though it was, I can think of no other reason. He can hardly have imagined that it suited him. In fact, the poor fellow must have looked perfectly ridiculous in it.'

'Yes, I agree, and that raises a question too. One for Frank, though. It must be years since you bought a hat, so you couldn't be expected to know what they cost now.'

'So that's the question, is it?'

'One of them. Another would be the size. Surely, if a man were buying a hat, for whatever purpose, he would automatically choose one in his own size?'

'And supposing it were a woman, pretending it was for her husband or gentleman friend?'

'It would come to the same thing. She would pretend to know the size, but she would be equally unlikely to get it exactly right.'

'So, if I understand you correctly, we are now assuming that our unknown murderer bought this hat and placed it beside Hugo after he had killed him. I know all about your passion for turning life into one long detective yarn, but isn't this making it unnecessarily complicated?'

'Not at all. It is always the psychological element which carries the most weight, you should know that by now.'

'And the psychological element here?'

'Hugo's meanness. If he'd set out to impersonate Gilbert, with the hat as a prop, he might have swiped the genuine article, or borrowed something from the wardrobe department which would pass; even laid out a couple of dollars in a second-hand store, maybe. But this one was new and bought in one of those gimmicky shops in Georgetown, than which nothing comes pricier. I could kick myself for not realising before that Hugo was simply incapable of lashing out to that extent. The most sublime practical joke ever invented would have lost its appeal if it had cost that kind of money.'

'Well, that may be true, but on the other hand, Tessa, why should anyone go to such lengths to make it appear that a practical joke was involved at all? Since it would inevitably appear that this was an ordinary case of robbery and violence, why all the fandango?'

'Because, if I'm right, this murderer was an amateur, new to the game and ignorant of the laws and police methods he would be up against. He or she may have hoped there would only be a formal enquiry before the case was closed, but they couldn't have relied on that.'

'With you on their track, I agree it would have shown a rather reckless complacency.'

'I won't rise because the real point is that they couldn't be sure that someone like Detective Meek wouldn't pop up and smell a rat, which made it necessary to take the extra precaution of planting evidence to suggest that the wrong man had been killed. Are you with me?'

'Oh yes, every step of the way.'

'So that, in the last resort, the police would have been conned into focusing their enquiries on such people who were known to be anti-Gilbert, agreed?'

'If you say so.'

'And there'd have been enough of those around to keep them occupied for weeks. Furthermore, they'd have heard all about Hugo's talent for mimicry in the first five minutes.'

'Whereas, in fact—'

'They should really be looking for someone with a motive for murdering Hugo.'

'And who might that be, I wonder?'

I sighed: 'Yes, it's a tough one, isn't it? And somehow I can't see poor old Frank making it on his own.'

CHAPTER SIX

INEVITABLY, the concept which I now accepted in principle, that Hugo's death had been deliberately planned and executed, brought a corresponding change of attitude. Until then it had been difficult to suppress a sneaking sympathy for the murderer and this had been the main impediment to whole-hearted co-operation with Frank. Knifing a man in the back and leaving him to die on a foreign pavement may not be a very nice thing to do, but I could think of no one whose behaviour had more consistently invited such treatment than Gilbert. Moreover, there was also the probability that his attacker had acted in a fit of blind rage or jealousy, without premeditation, but seizing the moment when it came and which, by unfortunate coincidence, happened to be during the lowest depths of the mood.

However, there must have been something more to it than this, for Hugo had not been a specially lovable character either and, pondering it in the solitude of my room, while Lorraine was out at work and even the piano silent, I came to the conclusion that my new born public spiritedness had sprung from the seed of self-preservation, with a passing salute to fair play.

So far as I could tell, there was not one of us who had nursed a particular grievance against Hugo, so it followed that his secret enemy had been clever and cunning both in concealing it and in planning the deed. That being so, there was really no way of telling whether he now regarded his mission as completed, or whether he would find it necessary to strike again.

These were not pleasant reflections and I was tempted to argue myself back into the belief that it was, after all, no more than a brutal crime of robbery and violence, committed by a stranger whose name I should never learn. In fact, I had almost succeeded in doing so, when unfortunately I remembered the hat.

'It was a size too large, I'd say,' Frank told me, champing away at his trough of raw vegetables and salami.

We were lunching at one of those places where you can eat as much salad as you please, for no extra charge, and taking full advantage of this he was already on his third helping.

'You'd say?'

'Well, there wasn't anything to compare it with. The gentleman didn't own any other hats, at least none that crossed the Atlantic with him; but that's the way it looked.'

'Didn't that strike you as odd? I mean, that he should have spent all that money on something which wasn't even a good fit?'

'In a way. It gave us the idea that it might have no connection with the crime at all, that someone could have dropped it there earlier on. Only that didn't seem too likely either, seeing it was only bought that morning. It wasn't until one of your people told us how Dunstan had this kink about impersonations that it began to make any sense. For that purpose he wouldn't have needed to be too particular about the size.'

'Who told you that?'

'Isn't it true? You mean he was such a nut that he would have to get even that kind of detail exactly right?'

'No, I mean which of us told you he was the kind of nut who liked to impersonate people?'

'Don't recall offhand. You want me to look it up?'

'Not really. It struck me that the murderer would be intent on getting that piece of information across to you, but on the other hand any innocent person could have come out with it too. It was the one thing we all knew best about poor old Hugo.'

Frank mumbled something unintelligible, his mouth too full of the last of the shredded cabbage to phrase the question or comment distinctly. When he had sorted this out, with the help of a quick gulp of pallid coffee, he wiped his mouth with the paper napkin, saying: 'Excuse me, please!' at the same time casting wistful looks at the salad table.

'Surely you've had enough, Frank? What were you going to say?'

'What? Oh, you mentioning "poor old Hugo" reminded me of something. He wasn't all that poor. Tell me this, Tessa; how much would an actor of his calibre rate, salary-wise?'

'Fifty a week during rehearsals,' I answered promptly, 'Two hundred in performance. Sterling, that is.'

'That's not too much!'

'It's never too much,' I agreed sadly, 'but it was more than he was accustomed to. Of course he'd have got some of his expenses on top of that.'

'And would have needed every cent?'

'Oh, dear me no, not Hugo. He was past master at cutting down on expenses. That's the other thing we all knew about him. Admittedly, he was living in quite a posh place in Georgetown, but he always put on a smart façade to impress people, and you can bet he was occupying a room in the attics and living off pizza and iced water, except when he could cadge a meal off someone. He was even less choosey about what he ate than you are, provided it was cheap.'

'So that could account for it.'

'For what?'

'His comparative affluence.'

'How do you know he was comparatively affluent?'

'Routine. He opened two bank accounts the day after he landed here. Both with the same bank, but one checking and one savings, at six percent interest rates. Two days before he died he made a cash deposit in that second one, amounting to four hundred dollars. Another thing, Tessa: these expenses you were speaking about, would he have drawn them in cash?'

'And to think I swallowed it when you told me there was to be no official investigation!'

'Oh, that's just one of the wheels that automatically start turning in a homicide case. You haven't answered the question.'

'Well, it would probably have been in travellers' cheques, but he could have cashed those anywhere, so it amounts to the same thing.'

'And you're not surprised to learn he had such a surplus he could afford to put nearly a thousand dollars in savings when he hadn't been in the country more than a week?'

'As much as that? Well no, I'm still not really surprised. I've told you what he was like and he could also have brought some sterling with him, to convert into dollars, thinking to get a better tax deal by investing it over here, or something. It was little dodges of that kind which so appealed to Hugo. Also he didn't strike me as the blackmailing type, if that's what you've been leading up to.'

'And just how many blackmailers have you come up against in your lifetime, Tessa?'

'Not many self-confessed ones, it's true, but one forms an image of such characters and Hugo was too brash and extroverted to match it.'

'Yet you maintain he was cunning and devious and loved money?'

'Yes, but saving money, rather than gaining it, which requires a different temperament. Besides I am sure a successful blackmailer would have to be extremely observant and intuitive and Hugo wasn't either of those things. He was fairly insensitive to other people's feelings.'

'Seems too bad to keep throwing your own words back at you, but you did say he had a genius for mimicry. Wouldn't that involve a degree of observatory and intuitive powers?'

'Honestly, Frank, I believe you've missed your vocation. You'd have made a howling success as one of those smooth Washington lawyers.'

'My folks couldn't afford to put me through law school. I did the next best thing and I don't regret it. Much.'

'No, I'm sure you're marvellous at your own job too. So if you have a hunch that Hugo was in the blackmailing game you may well be right. You're the expert.'

'No, I just put it forward as a possible motive and I wondered how closely you really knew him.'

'Not closely at all. He's someone who's been on the perimeter for ages, but this was the first time we'd ever worked together.'

'Which is how long? Five, six weeks?'

'About that.'

'And this would apply to the rest of the team? What I'm getting at,' Frank explained, driving his short stubby fingers through his short stubby hair, 'is that it would have needed sensational luck, in view of the character reference you've just given, to have dug his way into someone's confidence, or nosed out some information about them which they were trying their hardest to keep under cover, to have set up a blackmail operation based on that and to have got it in motion, all in a few weeks, right? Sensational luck, or some pretty thorough preparatory groundwork.'

'No,' I said thoughtfully, 'not necessarily either. I've never mentioned this before because I hadn't realised its significance, but the fact is that I have a peculiar position in the company; peculiar to me and Gilbert, that is, because neither of us belonged to the original cast.

The other four, and also the understudies and director, were together all through the London run. Gilbert and I only came in when that ended.'

I went on to explain how this had come about and in answer to Frank's next question I said:

'Oh, six months at least, more like eight; and there was a short provincial tour before that and before that rehearsals. Call it a year altogether. From my point of view, that's good news, isn't it?'

'Putting you in the clear as a possible blackmail victim?'

'Yes, which also applies to Gilbert, of course. Not that it alters anything. I've always known that I was innocent and I've never had much faith in Gilbert as a murderer either.'

'That so? Something gave me the idea that he wasn't entirely your favourite character.'

'Yes, but one mustn't allow prejudice to influence one's judgement and Gilbert is not at all the type to resort to physical violence. Besides, it would be unnecessary. If Hugo had been getting in his way, either by blackmail or any other means, Gilbert would have found far more subtle ways to settle his hash. His career would have folded so fast that by the time he realised what was happening he'd have had trouble getting the part of a spear carrier in the local pageant. Very few actors would sacrifice their careers in exchange for a regular income, from whatever source, as the record shows.'

'So we scrub Gilbert Mann?'

'For my money. There are so many small things, as well as major ones, to rule him out. I don't mean moral scruples. He might conceivably have run Hugo over in his Rolls-Royce, or ordered his chauffeur to do so, but he would never have put himself to the inconvenience of padding around and lying in wait. Except . . . except . . . except,' I added rather lamely.

'Except what?'

'Well, it's curious, but I never thought of it until this minute and I see now that I may have been looking at things from an entirely false point of view. I was so stuck with the idea of Hugo prancing down to the theatre dressed up as Gilbert that when that theory got thrown out I still went on accepting the only bit of factual evidence which supported it.'

'Yes?' Frank said in a prompting tone. 'Whose evidence?'

'Why Clive's, of course. I'd assumed all through that the man he saw diving down a side street was Hugo. But he never caught up with him and he never got near enough to see his face. He recognised him by the walk and by that blasted hat. But if Hugo wasn't wearing the hat, after all, where does that put us?'

'You tell me!' Frank suggested.

'No, I won't because I have a nasty feeling that you've known the answer all along.'

'There you go, piling it on again! As I see it, there could be two answers and you would be better than me at coming up with the right one. Either Clive did see Gilbert walking around the streets that night, or he didn't see either one of them, and that means . . .'

'That he invented it?'

'Or was genuinely mistaken. Would that make any sense?'

'I honestly couldn't tell you, Frank. Off stage, he's rather a dim personality and his whole life revolves round his beautiful and rather maddening wife. It's conceivable that the fear of losing her might have got such a grip on him that he was seeing hallucinations of Gilbert under every lamp post; but I can't think of any vendetta he might have had against Hugo.'

'Something to work on though?'

'You mean something for me to work on?'

'Or would you be afraid?'

'Certainly not. It wouldn't be the first time, as you know.'

'That's my girl I That's what I like to hear I And I'll be right in there behind you, don't forget, with all the most sophisticated modern techniques and American know-how ready to glide into action.'

I made a few suggestions as to what he could do with those, whereupon he practically choked himself with snorts of amusement and we sailed forth on to Pennsylvania Avenue, grinning like a couple of music hall comedians.

CHAPTER SEVEN

NO ACTION, of the gliding or any other variety, could be taken for the next twenty-four hours, because there was little to be gained and all to be lost by making myself conspicuous in seeking out members of the company before circumstances brought us together in the natural course of events. Moreover, with one entirely new addition to the cast, who had not even had time to learn his lines, an extra strain was imposed on our already ragged morale and the atmosphere was hardly conducive to bright enquiries, however subtly disguised, on the subject of hush money to the late Hugo Dunstan.

Clive and Jackie had been at the top of my list, since each had volunteered circumstantial evidence relating to the night of the murder, none of which had so far been corroborated, but it was virtually impossible these days to get five minutes alone with either of them, so concentrated were they on their reconciliation, and eventually I approached the problem sideways by prevailing on Toby to invite Catherine and Rose and myself to lunch in one of the Kennedy Center restaurants, where he was to engage Catherine's attention with all the charm and light banter at his command, leaving me and Rose to struggle on as best we could.

His consent to the plan was not given with tumults of enthusiasm, but when the time came he played his part with skill and verve and Catherine, who had no doubt found herself going rather short of adulation recently, expanded like a daisy in the midday sun. Nevertheless, there was no time for tactful beating around of bushes and as soon as the other two were fairly launched into their stride I asked Rose if she had bought any clothes in Washington. It seemed a reasonably innocuous question and too far from the knuckle to put her on her guard, but perhaps she was offended at being placed, as it were, below the salt, because she answered truculently:

'No, certainly not, they're far too expensive. Besides, why should I need to? I've brought everything with me.'

'You're lucky then. I never know what I need until I see it in a shop window.'

'One of those compulsive shoppers, I suppose. Personally, I find the whole business the most ghastly chore, particularly in those big stores where it takes forever to get served and they keep the temperature at boiling point. Kate and I spent a whole afternoon in one, looking for a present for my mother, and I was fit for nothing at the end of it. I had to go and lie down, or I'm sure I should have fainted.'

'Yes, the atmosphere can be rather oppressive. Those boutiques across the road are fun though. Have you tried them? They have some gorgeous things, not terribly expensive, and you can wander round for hours without having to set foot in the harsh, cold world.'

She did not rise of course, and her expression of polite boredom never wavered. Naturally, I had not expected her to blush and stammer, nor even make haste to change the subject, but the difficulty, as I was now being forced to recognise, both with her and with all my other suspects, was that I was dealing with professionals, trained actors and far too experienced to betray themselves by spontaneous reactions, once the personification of innocence had been assumed.

In the end, rather to my annoyance, it was Toby who broke down the defences, for having rattled through his own script he then took over mine. It happened right at the end of lunch, while he was waiting for the check and the conversation had become general again. Inevitably, there was some reference to Hugo and, seizing her chance to come out of obscurity, Rose treated us to one of her little homilies about the spread of violence, breakdown of law and order, etcetera. I could see that this was not making a very favourable impression on Toby and, glancing down at the slip of paper which had just been placed in front of him, he said casually:

'Oh, but none of that had any bearing on Hugo's death. Didn't you know?'

No one answered him, although our silence did not denote lack of attention, and he timed the business very expertly, digging for his wallet and slowly extracting half a dozen bills before continuing:

'According to this cop Tessa's become so chummy with, all the boys in the Homicide band are convinced that it was straight, pre-meditated murder. That clever little hat trick didn't fool them for a second. Isn't that right, Tessa?'

I presume he had not expected me to confirm it and Rose still did not utter a word either, but Catherine gave me a very sharp glance before rounding on Toby:

'Forgive me, my dear, but I think you must be talking nonsense. I daresay little Tessa misunderstood. Give me one good reason why anyone should have wanted to murder poor Hugo.'

'Very well, I will,' Toby replied, signalling to the waiter, who was hovering at a discreet distance. 'In a word, black-mail.'

Whereupon Rose began to tremble so violently that the cup she had been clutching slid out of her hand, dribbling coffee over the cloth, and a second later she collapsed forward on top of it.

'You can't honestly blame me,' Toby said, defending his behaviour that evening. 'You should never have drawn me in at all. I became so stultified with boredom listening to Kate telling me how to make a soufflé and how she's always wanted to play in Restoration. Frankly, I can't see that it matters. I gather they both require the light and frothy touch, so one would do just as well as the other.'

'That's all very well, but what about me?'

'You were the worst of all, sitting there so smugly, playing your little games at my expense and having rings run round you. I don't know where you expected that to get you.'

'I was following Frank's instructions. He's not going to be too pleased about this, I can tell you.'

'Oh, the hell with Frank!'

'Don't be silly, he's a dear.'

'Yes, and probably a very ambitious old dear, as well. If he believes there's the slightest chance that things are not so cut and dried as they appear, and if there was something in it for himself, it would be quite a clever move to get you to do the digging for him. On the other hand, I consider it more probable that he's simply stage struck and tickled to death to be playing secret games with a real live actress.'

'Yes,' I admitted, 'that had occurred to me too, but it's not on. He hasn't once suggested coming back stage, or asked me to introduce him to the stars and he hasn't even got a niece who collects autographs. Incredible as it may sound to you and me, he doesn't seem to be particularly interested in the theatre.'

'Then perhaps you should flatter yourself because I suppose the answer is that he fancies you. From the way you go drooling on about Robin, it wouldn't require a very acute brain to grasp that the conventional approach would get him nowhere; but to involve you in the pretence of hunting down a criminal would be right up your street.'

'I regard that as a fairly cynical statement, Toby.'

'I expected you to, but it is one which might bear a little reflection before you plunge me into any more expensive luncheon parties.'

I gave it a little reflection and then shook my head: 'No, I won't buy it. I'm sure Frank is on the right track and, much as I deplore your methods, you've more or less proved it. Admittedly, Rose is not very sound in wind or limb, but that hardly justified her going into a swoon when the word blackmail was mentioned.'

'So you take it as evidence of guilt? In that case, your job must be almost done and you should be grateful to me. You can hardly have expected it to be accomplished so speedily?'

'It's not over yet and I'm not grateful to you. You can't prosecute someone on the grounds that they blacked out at a luncheon party and, as far as I can see, all you've done is throw a big spanner in the works by putting her on her guard and letting it be known that the case is still open. The only hope was to lull everyone into a false sense of security.'

'My poor girl, you really are taking this to heart, aren't you?'

'I suppose I am. I may not have had much faith in it at the start, but, well, you know, Toby, you have to admit it was rather a strange way for Rose to behave and Catherine looked simply livid. There must be something behind it.'

'There now! You sound grateful, after all.'

'Perhaps it wasn't all bad, but it does call for a change of tactics and I shall have to tread much more warily in future. However, at least neither of those two will be in a hurry to spread the news that Rose fainted because of what you said. I expect they'll pass it off as the start of another migraine. God knows, she gets enough of them. Was it the same in London?'

'I really can't tell you. As you know, Catherine never missed a performance, so Rose's health was immaterial. Presumably, we should have noticed if she'd had both legs amputated, but I wouldn't care to bet on it.'

'Yes, it must be a humiliating position in many ways. I wonder how much she resents it?'

'Oh, as to that,' Toby said, 'how often have I warned you not to judge by appearances? People's true roles in life can sometimes be the exact opposite of those they put on for public display and we should all be thankful for it. Otherwise it would be a sad world for playwrights.'

CHAPTER EIGHT

1

I HAD almost forgotten Terry's predicament during the hiatus when we had all gone our separate ways and, remembering it at all it was with the assumption that his dismissal would have been shelved, in the face of these larger issues, and that at least Hugo's death would have brought a reprieve on that front.

However, I had underestimated Gilbert's single-minded tenacity. So far from relenting, he had actually profited by Mr Pattison's presence in Washington to settle the business and get the seal of disapproval well and truly stamped on Terry, who had orders to leave at one week's notice. The official excuse for this was that the postponement was already running the production into the red and cuts had to be made somewhere.

Considering his somewhat inflated opinion of his own worth, Terry had accepted the blow with resignation, showing defiance rather than disappointment and putting on quite a convincing act of having anticipated the decision and to some extent welcoming it.

'Shed no tears for me,' he announced when I attempted to condole. 'I saw which way the wind was blowing when they brought in Mr Muscle Man as my assistant. Assistant my Aunt Fanny! He's about as much use as a six months old baby. Not that I care! I'll be glad to get out, I'm here to tell you.'

'All the same, I'm sorry. I shall miss you.'

'You won't be the only one, I daresay, before they're through. There's more to this job than some people seem to realise and if they think they can hand it over to a bleeding amateur, just because he has a rich mum, they'll be in for a nasty old shock. Not my worry, though. The whole production stinks and if I'd listened to me own advice I'd have got out months ago.'

He was packing the contents of his desk at the time, and doing it with even more than his usual inefficiency, scattering papers around in the most reckless fashion and opening and closing the same drawer several times a minute. It suggested an element of bravado in all this fine talk and, exerting myself to show an interest in the subject nearest to his heart, I said:

'By the way, Terry, did those photographs ever turn up? You know, the ones you lost?'

'No, they didn't. I've searched high and low and in my lady's chamber, but not a smell of them. Not that it matters all that much. Like you said at the time, Jocelyn's got the negs safe in London. Don't know what induced me to get so het up about it, really; one more straw on the poor old camel's back, I suppose. If you ask me, there've been too many funny happenings around here. It'll be quite a relief to get back to sanity.'

'Well, I agree with you there, but, not wishing to sound unsympathetic, I suppose you wouldn't put that into the same category of funny happenings as Hugo's murder, for example?'

'God, no! I'm not raving mad, am I? It's just . . . well . . . as though there'd been some kind of a curse laid on us, if you can understand what I mean?'

'I'm not sure that I can.'

'Well, just think back for a minute and count up all the bad luck we've struck and you may get the message. First of all, there was my photographs; I'm not saying they were important to anyone but myself, but it was like a signal for everything to start falling apart, because just after that we had all the fuss with the bogus telegram from Daphne, which practically sent Gilbert off his nut and made life a hell on earth for the rest of us. Next thing is, you come in looking like death warmed up because your friend has been coshed with her own bicycle pump or whatever; so that makes everyone twice as gloomy as they were before and Miss Henneky gets a triple dose of the old migraine. So then Miss Fuller starts getting rattled and then . . . want any more?'

'No,' I replied thoughtfully. 'As you rightly said, I've got the message.'

'Well, there is more, as it happens, because, if you remember, it was about here that our two lovey doves fell out, which is something that has never been known before in all the annals of the world's great romances, and Clive goes lurching out into the night and gets lost between here and the Watergate. All this and murder too! Can you blame me for leaving without regrets?'

'Not when you spell it out, but tell me something else, while you're at it, Terry; do you trace any single connection between all these disasters?'

'You bet I do. It's the old jinx at work, that's what.'

'Oh, that's no help at all. I meant something tangible, that you could actually pin down.'

'So did I. I was referring to our own custom built witch, Miss R. Henneky. She's the most renowned Jonah in the business and she's got the old voodoo working for her again. That's my opinion, which I hand on to you free.'

I saw no point in trying to talk him out of it either. Superstitions not only die hard in the theatre, in a sense they are nurtured and cherished and the scoffers are liable to become unpopular if they voice their scepticism openly. It may well have been in flouting some ancient superstition that Rose had acquired her reputation in the first place. So instead of disputing the argument, I said:

'But all this mayhem is so recent. Just the last few weeks. You didn't have any trouble in London, did you?'

'Well, it's the kind of thing that always comes in waves, isn't it? For all I know, this one may have washed itself up on the beach now and you'll be in for some peace and quiet. Shouldn't depend on it, though.'

'But, listen, Terry, did you have any trouble in London?'

'We did and we didn't. I mean, every production has its ups and downs, doesn't it?'

'But nothing out of the way?'

'Nothing to compare with this lot.'

'So there you are! It sounds to me as though poor old Rose isn't your jinx at all; it's Gilbert. Apart from me, he's the only newcomer in the cast and it's only since he joined it that things have gone wrong. Nothing supernatural about it either. He was bent on throwing his weight about and making trouble and he's succeeded. Of course, I don't blame him for Hugo's death, or the attack on Lorraine, come to that, but nearly everything else, including the general malaise, can be traced straight back to him.'

'It's funny you should say that!'

'On the contrary, I'm perfectly serious.'

'Not funny in that way, but what you said reminded me of something. Do you know why he took over from Roger and why Roger opted out of the American tour?'

'Not precisely. Something to do with the Inland Revenue, I gather.'

'Too right! You have placed your tiny finger smack on the button.'

'There was no secret about it, was there?'

'No secret, duckie, just very, very sad news. He wanted to come here, you know, very much indeed, but he'd got himself into such a tangle that his accountants told him the only hope was to go and eat chocolate in Switzerland for six months. He just couldn't afford to risk getting soaked for double income tax.'

'Which of us could?'

'Roger could afford it less than anyone. Did you know that about a month before we closed he came a terrible purler on the Stock Exchange?'

'No, but it doesn't surprise me. He has the reputation of being a compulsive gambler.'

'You're so right, dear. His answer to that blow was to spend the next three weeks at the casinos, all night sittings, trying to win some of it back. Disastrous, I need hardly say.'

'Well, that was bad luck, but I suppose you don't seriously hold Rose responsible?'

'It's funny you should say that,' Terry said, a repetition which was now beginning to irritate me, specially as there was nothing remotely funny about it.

'The funny thing is, you see, Tessa, that it wasn't until you got me started on all this that things began to click, if you see what I mean? I knew about Roger's fatal plunge on the stock market, we all did, but he's a great old pro and he'd never let his private worries affect his performance, so it didn't really impinge, if impinge is the word.'

'And what impinges about it now? Please don't tell me it's funny I should ask that.'

'Well, it is, you know, no getting away from it, because I've just remembered that it was Rose who gave him the tip about the shares, which started all the rot.'

'Then I agree with you, for once; that really is a funny thing. I had no idea Rose took any interest in the stock market.'

'Oh yes, ever such a financial wizard in her small way. Spends hours totting it all up in the city pages when she's tucked away in Madam's dressing room. Only natural, I suppose. She'd need to have some hobby, poor old dear. Of course, you wouldn't have caught her at it because Wall Street isn't her scene and the financial pages here wouldn't have the same thrill.'

'And you mean to tell me that she's so knowledgeable that someone like Roger, who must employ armies of experts to look after his affairs, would actually follow her advice?'

'Without a doubt. He'd follow yours or mine, dear, if the stars said it was his lucky day, or he'd just seen three black cats walking backwards or something. That's what they mean by compulsive gambler. Jocelyn did an interview with a psychiatrist once on that very subject and he said that it's an addiction, just like drugs or alcohol, and although the poor things don't know it they suffer from this irresistible urge to put their money where they're bound to lose it. Deep down in the subconscious, they can't wait to get rid of the stuff. Shame, really!'

'Well, all I can say, Terry, is that if Roger was as far gone as that, he'd have found a way to lose his money, whatever happened, and therefore no blame attaches to Rose for having been the instigator on this occasion.'

'You don't think so? Well, I do. You might as well say that no blame attaches to someone who locks an alcoholic in a room full of gin bottles.'

This observation brought me by an obvious route to thoughts of Lorraine and a nagging little question which had come and gone, like an abortive sneeze at the back of the nose, started to tickle again. However, since I could neither bring it out nor completely suppress it. I tried to fasten my attention on the general theme.

'Incidentally, Terry, if it was Rose's tip which started this, I suppose she must have lost money too?'

'Yes, I believe she did, now you mention it. I seem to remember a bit of a whine going on. Doubt if it would be anything big though. She's too cautious to go in for the real plunge, for one thing and . . .'

'What?'

'Well, I don't imagine she has all that much to fling about, do you? Of course, naturally, I mean, I don't really know. She could be very well off, for all I know, and with her friend doing so well and everything . . .'

He burbled on in this strain for some minutes and I did not interrupt, for it suited me well. Sure enough, no sooner had the elusive little memory been pushed into second place than it bobbed up of its own accord and declared itself in its true colours. Terry's flow of speculation about Rose's income provided exactly the cover I needed to study its implications and I soon found that it was not only significant in its own right, but supplied the answer to several questions which had hitherto appeared unrelated and unanswerable.

Rather like a television announcer reading from an autocue, I assumed an earnest, attentive expression, while actually focusing on a point just above his head, in this case an electric clock, which gave out the news that it was now twenty-three minutes to twelve. In view of Frank's eccentric mealtime routine, I should have to look sharp if I were to catch him before he went out to lunch and, gathering up my bag and gloves in what I hoped was a leisurely fashion, I said:

'I must buzz now, Terry. Lorraine has to go up to New York this afternoon and I must try and catch her before she leaves. They've sent for her, just like that, out of the blue, and she's bound to have a million instructions for me.'

He looked rather hurt, so I poured some balm on the wound by asking whether there'd be a chance for another chinwag before he left.

'Doubt it, dear. I've got a few bits and bobs to straighten out here for tonight's dress rehearsal and then off to lovely old England in the morning. Anything you'd like me to take over for you?'

'No, thanks awfully, Terry, I can't think of anything.'

'Well, let me know if you have second thoughts. I'll be in and out this evening. Or if there are any messages you want carried? Always happy to oblige a mate. What about your old man, for instance?'

'No, really not,' I said, making great efforts to stifle my impatience. 'He's had all the news, actually. He called me at Lorraine's a couple of evenings ago.'

'Oh, I see. Okay, see you around, then!'

'Yes, goodbye, Terry. Take care and lots of luck!'

'Same to you, duckie. Something tells me you're going to need it.'

2

Taking no risks of being overheard, I walked through to the public foyer, which serves all three auditoriums at the Center and was on the same floor level as Terry's office. It is a vast, red carpeted hall, about the size of Paddington Station, stretching right down the entire length of the building and with at least fifty enormous, low slung chandeliers to add to its impressiveness. Going off at right angles is a similar, more modestly proportioned hallway, which is open to the public at all hours and does a brisk trade with out of town tourists. The various box offices, where I was happy to see a sizeable crowd waiting in line for tickets, together with sets of telephone booths, are set into alcoves along one side of this secondary foyer and it was one of these that I was making for. To reach it I had to pass close by one of the souvenir kiosks near the main entrance, where I saw a young man at the counter buying postcards. Something naggingly familiar about his back view caused me to look over my shoulder after I had passed and I saw that he had lost interest in his transaction and was watching me intently. Seen face to face, I recognised him instantly as Bob Mason, whom I had met in Frank's apartment on Sunday afternoon. In haste though I was, I could hardly cut him, since he had so obviously recognised me too and, while I hesitated, he dropped his handful of cards on to the counter and came towards me, uttering the inevitable:

'Hi there, Tessa! Nice to see you!'

Practice and one or two false moves in responding to this greeting had taught me that it was just as meaningless as our own 'How do you do?' and should be treated accordingly.

'Hi, Bob!' I said. 'Nice to see you!'

'I've just been buying tickets for me and Estelle to see your show. We can't wait.'

'Oh, good! I mean, I hope you'll find it was worth waiting for.'

'You bet we will. We're both crazy about the theatre. Go every chance we can get.'

'Oh, that's nice!'

'Musicals, drama, Shakespeare! You name it, we're there.'

'Oh, lovely! How's Frank?'

'Up to here,' Bob replied, passing a hand under his chin.

'Oh, why's that?'

'Been in Court all yesterday and today, giving testimony in a homicide case. The District of Columbia Superior Court, where it all happens. You visited there yet?'

'No, not yet.'

'You should give it a try, it's worth seeing. Get Frank to show you around one day when he's off duty.'

'What a good idea! Do you think there's any chance that he'd be off duty during the lunch break, if I were to take a cab down there now?'

Bob shook his head sorrowfully: 'You don't have to tell me you've never been there. It's housed in three separate buildings, for a start, and they have around forty Prosecutors' offices. I just don't see how you would ever be able to locate him.'

'Oh, damn! There was something . . . rather urgent I wanted to . . . well, ask his advice about.'

'Anything I can do?' Bob asked, sounding very kind and concerned.

'No, I'm afraid not, thanks all the same.'

'Well, hopefully, you could contact him at his home this evening. They haven't introduced all night sittings yet, so far as I know. You have the number?'

'Yes, but unfortunately we have our dress rehearsal tonight and another tomorrow, so there won't be much opportunity. Never mind, I'll think of something. Thanks again, Bob. At least you've saved me a useless telephone call. Bye for now, and I do hope you and Estelle enjoy the play.'

'We will, and you'll be great, I know it,' Bob said, in an earnest, emotional voice, making me feel like Ruby Keeler about to get her big chance.

Funnily enough, it was not until much later that it occurred to me that this passionate devotion to the theatre had come upon him rather suddenly, neither he nor his wife having evinced the faintest awareness of its existence when I was first introduced to them.

CHAPTER NINE

IT HAD become the custom, ever since acquiring sole use of the M.G., to go back to Georgetown for lunch on working days. It was only a ten minute run and well worth while for the change of ambience. If Lorraine was there too she usually made me one of her nutritious and peculiar sandwiches, consisting of rye bread, tuna and salad; when alone, I hacked myself a hunk of highly polluted, starch filled French loaf and piled it up with cholesterol in the form of butter and cheese.

On this occasion she was both there and not there, in the sense that her physical presence did not constitute the whole woman. Mentally, she was already half-way to New York and, with Muriel's help, was packing up rather more luggage than anyone else would have found necessary for a round-the-world trip. On the whole, this state of affairs suited me well, and not only for the sake of my bread and cheese. A more vital consideration was that the distrait mood promised a fair chance of prising out some spontaneous answers to one or two questions I was anxious to put to her and even that, from actual lack of conscious effort, some memory might be released which had hitherto been dormant. The principal snag was that Muriel was continually in and out of the room, fetching and carrying, enquiring whether this or that would be needed for the journey and once, at a particularly fraught moment, announcing that the cab was at the door.

'Then he must go away from my door,' Lorraine said irritably. 'I'm not half ready and he's much too early.'

'Well now, you know as well as I do, Miss Lorraine, Ma'am, it's going to take you all of one whole hour to get to Dulles airport.'

'Who said anything about Dulles? I'm going to New York, Muriel, not Glasgow. I get the shuttle from National and I can be there in fifteen minutes, minus. Listen, honey, there's some money in my coat pocket over there; be nice and go and pay him what we owe and tell him to call the office and say we need one in half an hour, right?'

'How long will you be gone?' I asked in the ensuing lull.

'Four nights, which is why I need to take so much stuff with me. And we finish up with a great big white tie and Ginger Rogers reception at the Museum, so I have to take four dinner dresses.'

'In order to skip off to the powder room four times during the festivities to change into a new outfit?'

'It's an idea, but it's mainly so I can decide which of them is the least horrible and dowdy when I get there. That way I won't give myself any excuse to go out and buy a new one. Will you be all right here on your own that long? Oh, my

God, what kind of a fool . . . ?' she exclaimed, all at once breaking off and looking up at me with a tragic expression.

'What's the matter now?'

'You are! How can I go and leave you here on your own? You'll be scared out of your mind!'

It was the opening I had been looking for and I said:

'No, I won't; on the contrary, you see, Lorraine . . .'

'Oh, don't give me that! Henry said you were shaking like a leaf those two nights I had to spend in the hospital.'

'Yes, I know, but the situation has changed since then. I've found out a number of things during the last few days and . . .'

At this point, Enter Muriel L, staggering under a huge bundle of horticulture, swathed in layers of thick cellophane.

'Call the airport and have them hold the plane for half an hour, will you?' Lorraine said a minute or two later, having battled with her finger nails and then her teeth in a futile attempt to tear aside all this pollution fodder.

Muriel took over with a pair of scissors from the dresser and expertly removed the flowers from their wrappings, then held them aloft in stunned silence. This quickly spread to me and Lorraine, for the bunch consisted of a dozen or more blooms, each the size of a soup plate, their colours shading from bright scarlet, down through coral and yellow to shell pink and white, the whole plaited up with streamers of red satin ribbon.

'Poinsettias, my God!' Lorraine muttered in a trembling voice as she tore open the little white envelope. 'Who the hell . . . ?'

'Henry?' I suggested.

'No, Henry would never dream up anything so vulgar. Besides, he knows I'm leaving town. JEEZus!' she added in a wail, staring incredulously at the square of pasteboard.

'Who was it, Lorraine? Who sent them?'

'Go and find a vase, would you please, Muriel? A bathtub might be the answer, if we have a spare one. Or, better still, look around for a grave stone. Here, see what you make of this, Tessa!' she said, handing me the card.

There were five words on it, which ran as follows: 'Get well soon, love Gilbert', and I said:

'There is only one thing you can make of it. Gilbert sends his love and wants you to get well soon.'

'That's a big help!'

'Well, to be fair, I suppose there is one other thing. The message is not in his handwriting, which means that he ordered the flowers by telephone and therefore they may represent the florist's taste and not his own. That's a point in his favour, anyway.'

'But why would Gilbert Mann be sending flowers to me? He doesn't even know where I live. It's in the phone book, but he wouldn't know me by that name.'

'I can explain that. He knows I'm staying with you, so all he had to do was to look up my address on Terry's list.'

'Oh well then, that clears everything up, no problem at all,' Lorraine said, looking as though this were indeed the case and immediately switching her attention back to the packing. 'That ghastly flowering forest was intended for you. Simple!'

'No, it wasn't. It couldn't possibly have been.'

'Give me one good reason why not? It didn't have my name on the envelope.'

'No, and you've said yourself that he doesn't know what it is. If he'd meant them for me, my name would be there all right, and furthermore he wouldn't be telling me to get well soon because he is perfectly aware that I have never been ill.'

'Oh, pooh! That was probably the florist's touch too. He thought plain old "love from Gilbert" wasn't warm and personalised enough and he tried to fancy it up. You'd better watch out though. You know what to look for when the Greeks come bearing gifts? Now, what else would I possibly need? Ticket? In my purse. Just check that for me, would you, honey? And listen, Tessa, I've been thinking and if you feel the slightest bit nervous you're to call Henry and tell him to get over here right away, this very minute, do you hear me? He loves you and he'll do anything in the world for you. Now, where the hell has Muriel got to? Oh, I know, disposing of your flowers. Well, I suppose I could be a big, brave girl and try closing these bags myself.'

So in the end she drove away without my having asked so much as one of the questions I had prepared for her and, with typical perversity, had actually contrived to raise a couple of new ones; such as whether Gilbert could conceivably have gone to so much trouble and expense for the express purpose of annoying her and whether her relationship with him had been exactly as she had described it on my first evening in Washington.

They were both quite unanswerable, so there was nothing for it but to cut my losses and set up some alternative lines of enquiry. 'Don't forget to call Henry!' had been Lorraine's parting words and there was just time to do so before I drove back to the theatre. It was not that I needed his support or guardianship because, as I had attempted to explain, I no longer had any qualms about being alone in the house. Nevertheless, I had a question or two for him as well and one of them related to the extradition laws. I got a straight answer too and he promised to call me back with further details in the morning.

Muriel put her head round the bedroom door during this conversation, waving and mouthing at me in a fashion which would have been quite meaningless had she not been wearing her hat and coat, signifying that this was farewell, and when I had rung off I had a fancy to see how she had finally disposed of Gilbert's flowers. Curiously enough, I could find no trace of them anywhere, although I searched all through the house, including the kitchen and bathroom and downstairs closet, and they were not in the dustbin either. The only conclusion was that she had stuffed them into her own shopping bag and this was a most unsatisfactory one. No one would have raised the slightest objection to her doing so, but the fact remained that Muriel had never been known to help herself to so much as a bristle from a toothbrush.

It was yet another small anomaly, which was to return intermittently to perplex me throughout the afternoon and add to the vague stirrings of apprehension which had beset me ever since the arrival of Gilbert's nasty, unsolicited gift.

CHAPTER TEN

1

THE curtain was due to rise on our second dress rehearsal at 7 p.m. and I do not imagine that any of us expected it to fall for the last time much before midnight. I only had one change and it was an easy one and even in normal running time my first entrance did not come for ten minutes. Nevertheless, and again like everyone else, I got to the theatre with two hours to spare, for on nerve racking occasions of this kind nothing soothes the queasiness so well as the peace and seclusion of the dressing room and getting down to business.

It was twilight when I pulled up outside the theatre, one of the most stunning times of the day in Washington, which boasts a larger share of visible sky than most cities and goes in for a spectacular line in sunsets. It is a fleeting time too though and, as I sat for a minute or two admiring the gold and crimson light reflected on the river, I noticed that away to my left the sky was rapidly filling with a huge black and purple cloud, obscuring the daylight, and felt the first menacing chill of an approaching storm. Unfortunately, before the sensation grew strong enough to get me moving again, I was struck by a far more uncomfortable one, just as strong but more nebulous in character. In short, I became convinced that as I sat there, silently observing the surroundings, someone else, close by, was silently observing me.

I had certainly heard enough about the perils of city life to have done the sensible thing, which was to slide out of the car and sprint across to the safety of the theatre and bribe someone to take the car down to the parking lot for me, but instead I turned as limp and weak-willed as if I had been pinioned in a steel trap, instead of my own silly funk.

How long this depressing state of affairs might have continued I cannot say, but luckily for me the spell was broken by the arrival of another car and the comforting sounds of slamming doors and human voices and I switched on the engine and manoeuvred myself down the ramp to the car park in the most cool and leisurely way imaginable.

Clive caught up with me at the exit.

'Jackie not with you?' I asked, experiencing another mild tremor of apprehension, for he looked rather cross and popeyed and the prospect of another quarrel looming was a most unhappy one.

Things were not as bad as that, it seemed, although relations were apparently somewhat strained, for he said irritably:

'She's here already. Forgot Teddy, if you please! I've been sent to fetch him.'

'Teddy who?'

'Oh, you know, that boring old cuddly toy who dogs our lives. I just hope to God he's turned up and then we can all go to sleep.'

'You've lost me again, Clive. I thought you'd been to fetch him?'

'Only because he wasn't in her dressing room, where she thought she'd left him. He's not at the hotel either; at any rate I couldn't find him and he's so repulsive that no one could possibly want to pinch him. Anyway, he's probably safe in mother's arms by now.'

'I do hope so, Clive. All these mysterious disappearances! I begin to feel there must be a kleptomaniac in our midst.'

'Really?' he asked in a puzzled tone, hovering outside Jackie's dressing room while I scrabbled for my key. 'You mean you've lost something too?'

'No, no, I was reminded of Terry's photographs, as a matter of fact. He never found them, you know.'

'Oh, I see! Well, too bad!' he said in a tone of utmost relief. 'For a moment I thought you were serious.'

'Terry took it very seriously.'

'I'm sure he did, my darling, but personally I consider that whoever removed those repellent photographs of the hideous old barn deserves a medal. A real public benefactor, in my considered opinion. Well, I must see if the old lady's had any luck with Teddy. Bye, love, see you later.'

Inevitably, this conversation had revived yet again the memory of the missing bouquet, only this time it brought another with it. It was as though by pushing open my dressing room door and stepping inside I had literally broken out of a wasteland of loose ends and futile speculation into a great burst of light, where all the outlines were sharp and clear. The sensation was so overpowering that I had to sit down and review the picture, detail by detail, to make sure that each one fell into its right place. At the end of five minutes I felt perfectly calm again and certain now, in my own mind, what had become of the missing flowers, who had stolen Terry's photographs and for what purpose and also, although this was just as much a formality as fitting the last section of blue sky into the jigsaw, why Hugo had been murdered and by whom.

It was not an unmitigated triumph, however, for as one door opens another shuts and my new insight also brought new responsibilities. One of them called for urgent and imperative action, if further disasters were to be averted, and I could not for the life of me imagine how it was to be accomplished. Debating whether to pick up the telephone and pass the job over to Henry, at the risk of being overheard on another extension, I paced about the room for a while and soon became fascinated, in a detached kind of way, to discover that real, hard, concentrated thought actually produced an audible drumming in the ears. It eventually dawned on me that the two things were in no way connected and that the drumming was not inside my head, nor even in the room. The navy blue and purple cloud which had excited my admiration when I saw it coloured by the light of the setting sun, was now getting down to business and all over Washington the drenching, saturating rain was teeming down. The heavens had taken charge and the matter was out of my hands.

2

Terry would have been gratified to learn how rapidly his departure ceased to be a matter of satisfaction or indifference and became a source of lament, for even the vile sandwiches he had rustled up for us would have been a banquet compared to Harrison's efforts in this department, which were non-existent. In fact, so far as we could make out, he had only waited for the curtain to rise on the dress rehearsal to leave the theatre, apparently under the impression that the hard day's slog was over.

The first act took just under two hours, which was an improvement on the previous evening, and there were only some relatively minor hold-ups. Nevertheless, it was almost nine o'clock when we broke for half an hour to allow for the set to be changed, and there was uproar and dismay when it was discovered that no supper had been laid on and that we were faced with the prospect of working far into the night without so much as a biscuit to sustain us.

Most unexpectedly, however, these grey skies were dispersed from my horizon almost as soon as they had gathered there. I had just resigned myself to joining Clive and Jackie in a trek across to the basement canteen when Catherine swooped down on me with the request that I should spare her a few moments in her dressing room, to go over a little business in my scene with her in the second act. I was working myself into a lather about this, wondering whether and in what fashion I had offended, when to my astonishment she gave me a nod which was not only as good as a wink, but was accompanied by a tremendously large one and I realised that I was actually being invited to share the private supper for the chosen few, which Rose was doubtless already setting out.

It was necessary to pass by my own door in order to reach Catherine's and I noticed the corner of a white envelope sticking out from underneath it. I managed to pull it all the way out and saw that it was a Western Union cablegram.

All thought of food, Catherine and anything at all except the white envelope in my hand instantly vanished and I became convinced beyond all argument that something terrible had happened to Robin and that in all essentials my life was now over.

Luckily, I managed to open it without tearing the contents to pieces because one glance at the message was enough to dispel the nameless fears and to restore my stomach to its right position. It had been despatched at 5.40 p.m. from New York and ran as follows:

'SOMETHING HAS CROPPED UP THIS END AND VITAL I SEE YOU STOP MEET ME NEAR END BAR MAIN FOYER WHEN YOU CAN GET AWAY STOP DO NOT REPEAT NOT LEAVE THEATRE LOVE LORRAINE.'

The relief was so overwhelming that I neither paused to question the sincerity or seriousness of these instructions, nor trouble myself over Catherine's invitation and the bad odour I should be in by ignoring it, nor even stop to remove my make-up. Lorraine often behaved eccentrically, but there was always a clear purpose behind her obscurest actions and silly jokes were simply not in her nature.

It did occur to me as I followed the circuitous route to the front of the house that it would have been simpler if she had found her way instead to my dressing room and waited there until I was free to talk to her, but then I remembered that this would probably have been ruled out by the risk of running into Gilbert.

Another delaying factor had been created by her choice of rendezvous, although this was something which she could not have foreseen.

The vast crimson and glass saloon, which has been described in an earlier chapter, is equipped in the most practical way imaginable, not with just a single large bar to enable only the most agile and alert among the audience to get a look in, as in so many London theatres, but with half a dozen small ones, spaced out at intervals of ten or twelve yards, providing all the customers with a fair chance. Moreover, although these amenities serve all three auditoriums, the timing of the shows is so arranged that none of them is filling up or emptying at the same time as either of the others. Thus, from the opening night onwards, our curtain would be up at eight o'clock and the interval start at nine-twenty, whereas in the Opera House next door each of these events would be staggered by half an hour.

Lorraine had unquestionably known this and therefore in choosing the bar at the furthest end of the room had seen it as the ideal environment to carry on a private conversation, without having to shout to make ourselves heard, and had certainly never envisaged any difficulty for myself in reaching it.

Unfortunately for these calculations, the average dress rehearsal differs from a regular performance in several respects and none more so than in its timing. As I entered from the Eisenhower side I was disgusted to find that the curtain had evidently come down only a few seconds earlier on the first half of the ballet programme which was playing next door, and that the audience was streaming down the wide, red carpeted stairs and flooding out over the hall. Since their potential number was anything up to two thousand and the great majority were moving directly across my path, I could see its taking a good five minutes to thread my way through to the other end, where Lorraine was presumably keeping her somewhat impatient vigil.

In fact, the journey was much more perilous than I had anticipated, for it is twice as hard to make a way between groups of people who are sauntering along in no special hurry than when they are moving in a purposeful manner and all at the same speed, and I found myself the object of some hostile and disapproving looks as I pushed my way through, apologising with every step. Admittedly, I must have looked rather absurd and ostentatious in full stage make-up, but there appeared to be some people who actively resented my attempts to by-pass them and positioned themselves in a way to obstruct me; or so I began to believe. There was even a little mild shoving and elbowing and, although fully aware that all emotions are contagious when a dozen or more are gathered together, I was still unpleasantly shocked, having reached the very heart of the crowd, by the prickly, panicky feeling that people were actually closing in on me, pressing up from behind, as well as barring my way forward. I tried to break out by moving sideways, but the same hostility seemed to prevail there and all at once I grew rigid, locked in the mad, hysterical fear that all these well dressed, well heeled ladies and gentlemen, fresh from the sweet and civilised delights of Coppélia, were about to turn on me and perform a lynching.

Powerless to move an inch of my own accord, I yet found myself, only seconds later, stepping forward, and quite rapidly, in the direction I was bound for. It was as though some stranger in the crowd, sensing my fear and knowing it to be well founded, had taken charge, gripping my arm with one tight, steely hand and pressing the other flat against the small of my back, so that I was propelled along like a rubber toy.

I could hear a minor hubbub going on in the background, but it was growing fainter and in no time at all the groups of people became fewer and more widely spaced, so that it was easy to carve a way through without making physical contact. I was able to turn my head slightly, to look at my partner in this weird dance and, since by this time everything around me had become so totally unreal, I was not particularly stunned to see that it was Estelle Mason.

In the intervals between fetching the children from barbecues and dropping by on her arthritic mother-in-law, she must have found time for a few karate lessons because my right arm and shoulder had become completely immobilised in her steely, competent grip. However, I did not complain about this because I had never doubted that the exercise was saving my life and almost immediately, as the pace slowed down, she confirmed the fact herself:

'Sorry to be so informal,' she said, 'but someone back there was after you with a knife. Don't worry, Bob has it all under control.'

Several questions sprang to mind, but for some reason the words eluded me and, before I could dig them out, one had already been answered. We had travelled right up to the far end of the hall, past the last chandelier, to the secluded corner where Lorraine had told me to meet her; only, needless to say, she was not there.

CHAPTER ELEVEN

'ALL due to Frank, you know,' I told Toby over a late supper the following evening. 'No wonder I love the fuzz!'

Our first night, contrary to most expectations, though not, as it happened, to the time honoured rule, had been a roaring success and even allowing for the partisanship of all first night audiences, hopes were running high. It was true that, between kisses, Andy had remembered to call a rehearsal at ten in the morning, but for a few brief hours we felt free to bask on our laurels, a luxury enhanced in my case by the fact that, as Lorraine had once remarked of Gilbert, I was still alive to enjoy it.

'Not forgetting Bob and Estelle,' I added. 'They were both cops themselves until they got married and Bob went into the family dry cleaning business. Did I tell you that?'

'Yes, I believe you did,' Toby admitted. 'I can't quite remember how often.'

'But Frank was the true blue hero of the hour. He was so concerned about my safety that he actually delegated

Bob and Estelle to keep an eye on things when he knew he wouldn't be available. Wasn't that sweet?'

'Yes, very considerate,' Toby agreed.

'They were rather lacking in finesse, poor loves! When Frank arranged for us all to meet at his flat he tried so hard to pass it off as a jolly social occasion, but Bob and Estelle stayed just long enough to note my height, weight and distinguishing marks, before bounding off into the night. Still, what does that matter? They were both on hand when the balloon went up and that's what counts.'

'Had you warned Frank that it might?'

'I tried to, as soon as Terry let the cat out of the bag, but I ran into Bob and he told me that Frank was in court. Why do you keep looking at your watch, Toby?'

'Because I'm tired.'

'You're joking! I feel I could go on all night.'

'You have gone on all night. It is now three a.m.'

'What does that matter? We can't go to bed until the papers come, in any case.'

'You're wound up, Tessa, that's your trouble. All right for some, but I lost that key years ago.'

'I don't believe you're tired at all,' I said accusingly. 'You not only keep looking at your watch, you also keep looking at the door. Now why should that be?'

'Oh, stop nagging! Get on with your story, if you must, but allow me to look where I please. I suppose you suspected Terry all along, otherwise you wouldn't have pounced when he made his fatal error?'

'It was more a cumulative thing, really. I think he had started to lose his head quite early on, even before the attack on Lorraine. I suppose the fuss over the photographs was the first hint.'

'Then you're cleverer than I thought. Knowing Terry, I should have been surprised if he had not made a fuss, specially in view of what the photographs revealed.'

'I agree, but this was an untypical fuss, just one wild outburst and then it all petered out. Normally, he would have gone squeaking on for days, but he must soon have seen that as long as those photographs remained out of his possession he was in real trouble and his best chance was to lie low until he'd completed his plans to get them back. That was when his behaviour became so fantastically strange and irresponsible.'

'Indeed? I can't say I noticed.'

'Yes, you did; you remember perfectly well how often he was missing when he was needed and how furious it made Gilbert. There was a heavy clue there because Terry must have realised that his job was already pretty shaky, but of course everything had to go by the board until he'd got his photographs back and what appeared to be incompetence was really part of a carefully arranged campaign to search the premises of all the people who might have taken them. What puzzled me was that he should have left out Rose; or, to be precise, that he hadn't started with Rose.'

'Why did you expect him to?'

'Because she was his current victim. And you know something, Toby? I actually saw him going to work on her on my first day in Washington. I was on the escalator at the Hirschorn and I saw Rose and Terry sitting close together on a couch. I took it for granted that Catherine was prowling about somewhere just out of sight and that they'd bumped into each other by accident, but when you think of it that was pushing coincidence a bit far. Terry's no culture fiend, for a start, and the expression on Rose's face should have warned me. It wasn't just bored or impatient, she looked absolutely stricken and it was soon afterwards that she got her first bad migraine attack, so I feel sure that Terry had met her there by appointment, to put the screws on, which was why he never attempted to search Catherine's apartment.'

'But wouldn't they have been the obvious people to have taken the photographs?'

'Yes, naturally; in which case they would have destroyed them instantly. That would have set him back, but it wouldn't have been half so disastrous as if someone else had got hold of them and meant to hang on; that's to say, someone who recognised the significance of that extra little set of prints, which had nothing whatever to do with a barn in Provence. So I think the plan was to take each of the rest of us in turn, starting with the easiest.'

'Who was Andy, I suppose?'

'Yes, Terry could always produce a legitimate reason for getting into his room. My guess is that he was on his way back from there when I met him in the street, although he had the cheek to pretend not to know where Andy was staying. That was a blunder because they'd spent a whole week here together before the rest of us arrived, so he must have known. Anyway, to use his own word, it didn't impinge at the time and I led him there by the hand, which resulted in his getting to know the exact location of Lorraine's house, and so making me number two on his list. However, I also drew his attention to the M.G., which was very nearly his undoing.'

'Was it really?'

'You see, it's a very distinctive old motor, practically rates as a veteran here and terribly easy to recognise. Where he went wrong, apart from mixing up our bedrooms and wasting a lot of time in Lorraine's, was in assuming that she was one of those conventional Americans who never move a yard on foot. By this reckoning, when the M.G. was parked by the kerb she was at home and when it wasn't she was out. Dead simple! Furthermore, once inside the house he believed that he only had to keep one eye trained on the street to get a clear warning of her return, in which event he would have galloped downstairs and out through the garden. When he'd satisfied himself that I hadn't got the photographs and there was still no car outside, he thought he had all the time in the world to leave by the front door and put the key back under the urn. He had no means of knowing that the car was at the garage for overhaul and that Lorraine was using her bike.'

'Which reminds me, Tessa: how was it that he was able to get past the bike to let himself out, when it so effectively prevented your getting in?'

'Well, he's quite a skinny creature and presumably he managed to hold it back just far and just long enough to squeeze through; and then it toppled sideways again when he shut the door. Any more objections?'

'Yes, one more,' Toby replied. 'You told me in strictest confidence and on pain of death that Lorraine was certain the man who attacked her was black.'

'I know and I'm afraid that inadvertently I was responsible for that mix-up too. When Terry saw my taxi driver he was knocked sideways for a moment, but later he realised that if a black man wearing a scarlet cap could give the momentary impression of a red-haired negro, the same trick could be used in reverse. By putting his coat collar up and concealing most of his head under a black woolly cap he could probably ensure that any witness who did come forward to say he'd seen him enter or leave the house would be almost bound to describe him as black. I'm not making all this up, you know. I got it from Frank, who's in charge of the grilling, and up for promotion, I daresay, the way Terry's been pouring it all out.'

'I never thought for a moment that you were making it up. What would be the point?'

'I just wondered why your attention kept straying. Aren't you interested in what I've been telling you? You should be because it provides some fascinating slants on human nature, which you ought to take note of, if you're to stay in business. For instance, although Terry was tireless in devising ways and means to carry out his programme, he was extremely limited and repetitive when it came to the actual props. Two hats, you notice; and of course two telegrams.'

'Two?'

'I'm including the one he sent to me yesterday, signed Lorraine. I confess that it fooled me. I suspected he knew the game was up and escape the only thing left to him. Incidentally, wasn't he lucky to have got the sack anyway and was able to fade out so unobtrusively? I'm sure he could have stayed on if he'd put up a fight, but naturally it suited him much better this way and I'd worked it out that he'd see the uselessness of going to England, so long as I was around to tell the tale, because of the extradition laws. I thought he'd make for Brazil or one of those, which was why I telephoned Henry and asked him to alert Frank. My mistake was in not seeing that Terry wasn't quite ready to pack it in and that, having failed to blow my head off with the explosive in the poinsettias, he then took a ticket for London, via New York, where he stopped off long enough to bait the trap with the telegram and then caught the shuttle service back to Washington for the last desperate throw.'

'Desperate is the word,' Toby said. 'That bomb in the flowers, for instance; it was much more likely to have blown Lorraine's head off, and where would that have got him?'

'But, you see, Muriel had ordered her cab much too early, so it arrived and waited outside the house for a few minutes and then drove away again. If Terry was waiting at a safe distance to dump the flowers he would have concluded that Lorraine was inside it, leaving only me to disentangle all those ribbons. One rather amusing sideline was the way they disappeared so mysteriously, but I should have remembered how literal minded Muriel is. When Lorraine suggested dumping them on a grave she did exactly that. Obvious, really, since there happened to be an old burial ground at the bottom of the garden. Now you're looking at the door again! I do wish I knew why. Are you expecting someone?'

'Only the papers and as soon as they come you know where I'll be off to, don't you? So you had better make the most of the time that remains and tell me about the other telegram. Was it the one Gilbert got from Daphne?'

'Right. I expect Terry's friend, Jocelyn, was the accomplice on that. There was a dicey moment when it looked as though Terry would be sent to the airport to meet her, but in the end Gilbert thought better of it and went himself. He even gave Terry a key to his hotel suite, so that he could strew it with flowers, which provided a better opportunity than he could have dreamed of to search for the photographs. Of course he didn't find them, so Hugo was the next to be given the treatment and we know what happened there?'

'He got a message saying rehearsals had been cancelled for the whole day?'

'It was clever thinking because, if things hadn't worked out, Terry had only to deny that he had sent it and no one would have had any reason to disbelieve him. Also he must have guessed that when Hugo's absence became crucial he would be the obvious person to be sent to the hotel to rout him out. I suppose when he got there and found all the ghastly photographs of the Provençal barn quite intact, but no little special folder containing the blackmail material, he realised that Hugo had understood its significance and was carrying it about with him. So the only way for Terry to get it back was to lie in wait, then follow him down to the theatre and knife him in some deserted side street. He even had the forethought to trot round the corner first and buy a Gilbert type hat, to confuse the issue. He spared no pains, you have to admit that.'

'I admit nothing. It was all in extremely bad taste and very selfish as well. Not a thought for the play, you notice! I almost wish I had taken away his nasty photographs myself. I might have, if I had known how easy it would be. What lunacy to keep them where he did!'

'Oh, do you think so? Personally, I call that rather clever. The victims would have reasoned just as you did, never dreaming that one of those dreaded little folders contained all the damning evidence; whereas the rest of us went out of our way to avoid having to look at them. All except Hugo, of course. I suppose he took them as a preliminary move in some practical joke he was setting up, with no idea at all of what he was really getting his hands on.'

'Does anyone know what that was? Do you?'

'Not until this morning, when I had my little talk with Rose. She's more relaxed about it now and terribly on my side because she believes it's due to me that Frank has promised that the relationship won't be made public, if and when they catch up with him.'

'Catch up with whom, for God's sake?'

'A boy named Patrick Henneky. You may remember, Toby, that about six months ago there was quite a sensational bank hold-up somewhere out in California, which was the work of terrorists calling themselves the something or other liberation movement. They mowed down everyone in sight and got away with about half a million dollars, but there were automatic cameras clicking away throughout the operation and the police got some good pictures of individual members of the gang, which they then circulated to the newspapers. One of them was a young man who has never been identified, except by Terry that is, who recognised him as Rose's son, Patrick.'

'What an extraordinary coincidence!'

'Plus sharp observation and a good memory. He'd worked in the Welfare Service at one stage of his career and he came across Patrick when he'd been sent down for taking part in a bank robbery in England. When his sentence was over Patrick disappeared and neither Rose nor anyone else knew what had become of him until he turned up in this photograph. You can see that it wouldn't have been very nice for Rose, or Catherine either, if the news had got around.'

'No, very annoying for them. I am so glad you fixed him.'

'I haven't yet discovered what hold he had over Roger, but I bet he was fleecing him too, and it was probably some little oversight on Roger's part which would have got him into deep trouble with the Inland Revenue.'

'That wouldn't surprise me,' Toby said. 'It had got to the point where the subject had become an obsession with him. He was a dreadful bore about it, poor old Roger!'

'Of course, as soon as Terry realised how he'd given himself away, he tried desperately to cover his tracks by thrashing around in all directions, and he started on about Rose being a jinx and causing Roger to lose a packet on the stock exchange, among other childish nonsense. As though anyone would follow Rose's advice about anything, least of all the stock market!'

'Which reminds me, Tessa; I suppose I have to ask you this, otherwise it will be like depriving you of the biggest strawberry on the plate, which you'd been saving for the last mouthful. Just how did Terry give himself away?'

'Oh, it was just some reference he made to Lorraine's bike when she got knocked on the head. He shouldn't have known that. Lorraine was so distraught about its being, as she believed, a poor downtrodden, victimised black man who'd attacked her that she made me swear on my oath to shut up and not give out any details at all. And, after all, my strawberry seems to have had a rotten centre,' I complained after a slight pause, 'you are looking at the door again and not listening to a word I say.'

'Yes,' he admitted, 'and here, coming through it, is some more of your beloved fuzz. I wonder what this one wants? Not me, by the look of it. I shall . . .'

It was now my turn to switch off, for he was absolutely right. A tall, fair-haired man, looking strangely like a recently promoted Chief Inspector, who had been married for approximately five years and two months, had just entered the restaurant, and I knew exactly who he was tailing.

THE END

FELICITY SHAW

THE detective novels of Anne Morice seem rather to reflect the actual life and background of the author, whose full married name was Felicity Anne Morice Worthington Shaw. Felicity was born in the county of Kent on February 18, 1916, one of four daughters of Harry Edward Worthington, a well-loved village doctor, and his pretty young wife, Muriel Rose Morice. Seemingly this is an unexceptional provenance for an English mystery writer—yet in fact Felicity's complicated ancestry was like something out of a classic English mystery, with several cases of children born on the wrong side of the blanket to prominent sires and their humbly born paramours. Her mother Muriel Rose was the natural daughter of dressmaker Rebecca Garnett Gould and Charles John Morice, a Harrow graduate and footballer who played in the 1872 England/Scotland match. Doffing his football kit after this triumph, Charles became a stockbroker like his father, his brothers and his nephew Percy John de Paravicini, son of Baron James Prior de Paravicini and Charles' only surviving sister, Valentina Antoinette Sampayo Morice. (Of Scottish mercantile origin, the Morices had extensive Portuguese business connections.) Charles also found time, when not playing the fields of sport or commerce, to father a pair of out-of-wedlock children with a coachman's daughter, Clementina Frances Turvey, whom he would later marry.

Her mother having passed away when she was only four years old, Muriel Rose was raised by her half-sister Kitty, who had wed a commercial traveler, at the village of Birchington-on-Sea, Kent, near the city of Margate. There she met kindly local doctor Harry Worthington when he treated her during a local measles outbreak. The case of measles led to marriage between the physician and his patient, with the couple wedding in 1904, when Harry was thirty-six and Muriel Rose but twenty-two. Together Harry and Muriel Rose had a daughter, Elizabeth, in 1906. However Muriel Rose's three later daughters—Angela, Felicity and Yvonne—were fathered by another man, London playwright Frederick Leonard Lonsdale, the author of such popular stage works (many of them adapted as films) as *On Approval* and *The Last of Mrs. Cheyney* as well as being the most steady of Muriel Rose's many lovers.

Unfortunately for Muriel Rose, Lonsdale's interest in her evaporated as his stage success mounted. The playwright proposed pensioning off his discarded mistress with an annual stipend of one hundred pounds apiece for each of his natural daughters, provided that he and Muriel Rose never met again. The offer was accepted, although Muriel Rose, a woman of golden flights and fancies who romantically went by the name Lucy Glitters (she told her daughters that her father had christened her with this appellation on account of his having won a bet on a horse by that name on the day she was born), never got over the rejection. Meanwhile, "poor Dr. Worthington" as he was now known, had come down with Parkinson's Disease and he was packed off with a nurse to a cottage while "Lucy Glitters," now in straitened financial circumstances by her standards, moved with her daughters to a maisonette above a cake shop in Belgravia, London, in a bid to get the girls established. Felicity's older sister Angela went into acting for a profession, and her mother's theatrical ambition for her daughter is said to have been the inspiration for Noel Coward's amusingly imploring 1935 hit song "Don't Put Your Daughter on the Stage, Mrs. Worthington." Angela's greatest contribution to the cause of thespianism by far came when she married actor and theatrical agent Robin Fox, with whom she produced England's Fox acting dynasty, including her sons Edward and James and grandchildren Laurence, Jack, Emilia and Freddie.

Felicity meanwhile went to work in the office of the GPO Film Unit, a subdivision of the United Kingdom's General Post Office established in 1933 to produce documentary films. Her daughter Mary Premila Boseman has written that it was at the GPO Film Unit that the "pretty and fashionably slim" Felicity met documentarian Alexander Shaw—"good looking, strong featured, dark haired and with strange brown eyes between yellow and green"—and told herself "that's the man I'm going to marry," which she did. During the Thirties and Forties Alex produced and/or directed over a score of prestige documentaries, including *Tank Patrol*, *Our Country* (introduced by actor Burgess Meredith) and *Penicillin*. After World War Two Alex worked with the United Nations agencies UNESCO and UNRWA and he and Felicity and their three children resided in developing nations all around the world. Felicity's daughter Mary recalls that Felicity "set up house in most of these places adapting to each circumstance. Furniture and curtains and so on were made of local materials. . . . The only possession that followed us everywhere from England was the box of Christmas decorations, practically heirlooms, fragile and attractive and unbroken throughout. In Wad Medani in the Sudan they hung on a thorn bush and looked charming."

It was during these years that Felicity began writing fiction, eventually publishing two fine mainstream novels, *The Happy Exiles* (1956) and *Sun-Trap* (1958). The former novel, a lightly satirical comedy of manners about British and American expatriates in an unnamed British colony during the dying days of the Empire, received particularly good reviews and was published in both the United Kingdom and the United States, but after a nasty bout with malaria and the death, back in England, of her mother Lucy

Glitters, Felicity put writing aside for more than a decade, until under her pseudonym Anne Morice, drawn from her two middle names, she successfully launched her Tessa Crichton mystery series in 1970. "From the royalties of these books," notes Mary Premila Boseman, "she was able to buy a house in Hambleden, near Henley-on-Thames; this was the first of our houses that wasn't rented." Felicity spent a great deal more time in the home country during the last two decades of her life, gardening and cooking for friends (though she herself when alone subsisted on a diet of black coffee and watercress) and industriously spinning her tales of genteel English murder in locales much like that in which she now resided. Sometimes she joined Alex in his overseas travels to different places, including Washington, D.C., which she wrote about with characteristic wryness in her 1977 detective novel *Murder with Mimicry* ("a nice lively book saturated with show business," pronounced the *New York Times Book Review*). Felicity Shaw lived a full life of richly varied experiences, which are rewardingly reflected in her books, the last of which was published posthumously in 1990, a year after her death at the age of seventy-three on May 18th, 1989.

Curtis Evans